THE BISHOP'S TREASURE

ALSO BY BRENT TOWNS

THE BISHOP'S TREASURE

A BROOKE REYNOLDS AND MARK BUTLER STORY

BRENT TOWNS

ROUGH
EDGES
PRESS

Rough Edges Press
An Imprint of Wolfpack Publishing
701 S. Howard Avenue 106-324
Tampa, FL 33609

roughedgespress.com

Paperback ISBN 978-1-68549-708-8
eBook ISBN 978-1-68549-349-3
LCCN 2023948372

"We will go down in history either as the world's greatest statesmen or its worst villains."
—Hermann Göring

THE BISHOP'S TREASURE

SCHMIDT FOUNDATION

Johann Schmidt: 62, Founder of the Schmidt Foundation, German

Mark Butler: 25, Field agent, American

Brooke Reynolds: 32, Head of Security, American

Molly Roberts: 22, Electronic Researcher, British

Werner Krause: 28, Historian, German

Isabella Pavesi: 22, Artifacts, Italian

Mr. Webster: 19, Computer Geek (Hacker) Country of Origin, Unknown

Grace Cramer: 29, Document Investigator, Australian

THE BEGINNING

The Golden Hawk, 1672

There was a heavy sea mist hanging over the steel-gray Atlantic, enveloping the Spanish treasure galleon, *Golden Hawk* returning to her mother country from the Caribbean with her hold stuffed with valuables. Sometime during the night, after the fog had settled in, they had lost their escort, two smaller galleons, both with 20 guns. Not that the *Hawk*, as she was known, couldn't look after herself for she was armed with 40 cannons of various sizes.

On the halfdeck, Captain Alejandro Garza paced, lines of worry on his face. He'd been at it since before dawn when the watch officer had roused him. Stopping suddenly to peer into the mist, he strained to listen at the rail. He'd lost count of how many times he'd done it, thinking he'd heard something.

"If you don't stop pacing, Alejandro, you will wear a hole in the deck," a voice said from behind him.

Garza turned to see Bishop Torres standing there, resplendent as always in his fine robes.

"Let me worry about that, your grace."

Torres shrugged. "As you wish. Is there any sign of the other ships?"

"No."

"I'm sure Captain Ortega and Captain Morales aren't far away."

"It's not them that I worry about. It's what the fog hides that I can't see."

Piercing the cold morning air, the sudden boom and beating of deep-throated drums shook both men to the core. "What is that?" Bishop Torres asked apprehensively.

"That, sir, is the sound of cannon." Garza hurried towards the rail of the half-deck. "All hands, action stations. Load all guns and run them out. Hur—"

A sudden break in the fog briefly revealed to Garza a horrific scene. Two smaller galleons, his escorts, were locked in battle. Not with an enemy, but with each other. It appeared as though one was already dismasted. Morales's ship. It also looked to be on fire.

Then the two warring beasts were enveloped by the fog, disappearing once again.

Garza stepped back, stunned by what he'd just witnessed. He turned to Torres. "Please, go below, your grace."

"What is happening, Alejandro?" the bishop demanded.

"I do not know."

"You must turn the ship elsewhere," Torres said. "We must get the treasure as far away as possible."

Yes, the treasure. Gold and silver coins, jewels, tapestries, rings, fine plates, gold, and silver ingots. The collection was priceless, yet not worth one man's life. And yet it was an all-encompassing thought for those who knew.

Garza's second in command appeared, Teniente

Molina. The captain remained calm and said, "Get everyone aloft that you can spare, Teniente. I want more sail. We have to catch some wind if we are to get away from this treachery."

The officer snapped to attention. "Yes, sir."

More orders were barked, and men scurried about the galleon's rigging, doing their utmost to give the *Hawk* its best chance of getting away. Garza moved to the rail and raised his eyeglass.

"What do you see?" the bishop asked as he stood one pace behind the captain.

"Nothing, but I can still hear them."

Torres strained his ears and caught the faint sound of human cries, eerie as they drifted through the fog.

Garza lurched, catching himself. He looked up at the *Hawk's* sails and saw them filling. They'd caught a breeze. His unease, however, remained. Ortega's ship was still faster than the *Hawk* and would catch her if given the chance. Garza's only chance was that Morales could stay engaged long enough to enable the *Hawk* to get beyond the horizon.

Or he could engage.

"Do not think about it, Alejandro," Torres responded as though reading the captain's mind. "The treasure comes first, unless we are directly engaged."

"Sir, we are starting to make good headway," Teniente Molina said enthusiastically.

Garza could feel the surge beneath his feet, the roll of the ship. He turned to his coxswain. "Timonel, bring the ship around to the east on the compass."

"Sir."

Molina looked at his captain. "Sir? I do not understand."

"Once we are out of this fog, Teniente, we will be in the open. I'm hoping that Ortega and Morales will be locked together long enough for us to get below the horizon. Even then, I am hoping that Ortega presumes that we have continued on our route north. If we go east, then we have a chance of losing him."

"I understand, sir."

"Good. Now, see that the gun crews are prepared just in case."

Molina disappeared below the deck, leaving Garza to himself. Except he wasn't. The bishop came up beside him and said, "We need to get back on our original course, Alejandro."

"You heard the reason why we can't, Your Grace."

"And I'm telling you that we need to."

Garza stared into the eyes of Bishop Torres and saw the man he knew was inside. He'd heard the stories from the new colony. The bishop was a harsh, cruel man. He'd whipped slaves to death on a whim. Slept with the daughters of important people, and others who were not. All because the position he held gave him the power to do so.

"Your Grace—"

"Back to our previous course, Alejandro, or I shall have you relieved."

Garza turned and shouted, "Prepare to come about! Steer original course. God have mercy on us all."

Activity picked up and the *Hawk* started to heave her great bow around. Garza felt the breeze pick up even more, and on it he thought he caught the cries of battle again.

From the stern, with full sails, the *Golden Hawk* was a magnificent sight. And as she disappeared into the fog, the treasure ship sailed into oblivion.

————

The Mediterranean, One Month Ago

"Captain, they are boarding us. We must do something," the first officer of the *Venetian Sea* said urgently.

"What is it that you propose that we do?" asked Captain Moreno. "Spit on them?"

"But you know what they are after. It can only be one thing."

"Of course it's only one thing," Moreno snapped as he watched the armed intruders come over the side of his vessel. "I knew it was a bad idea right from the outset."

The *Venetian Sea* was on her penultimate voyage, her last being to the scrap yard in Indonesia. However, before that could happen, his mission was to make a delivery to India, in the form of nuclear waste. Moreno had set course from Spain to Suez the day before and now was in the middle of the Med, under attack by…pirates!

"How can there be fucking pirates out here?" he asked aloud.

His eyes widened as he saw a large person on the deck point his weapon toward the bridge structure. The weapon discharged and bullets punched through the wheelhouse glass. Moreno dropped to the deck, hands over his head. His first officer fell beside him, eyes wide, blood pouring from his mouth and throat where two misshapen bullets had torn flesh.

The other officers on the bridge dropped to the deck as well, crying out in alarm. Moreno closed his eyes, wishing he was somewhere else.

"Captain, do something!" another officer called to him.

"Just stay down," he shouted back. "Let them get what they came for and they will be gone."

Moreno wasn't sure whether he believed that or not. The only other time he'd had experience with pirates was off the coast of Somalia. In that instance his employer could afford to have security teams guarding the deck. But *Venetian Sea* was headed to the scrap yard. There was no security team. Just his crew. They weren't supposed to be carrying any cargo.

Then they were.

Now this.

The shooting stopped and Moreno climbed cautiously back to his feet. He peered down at the deck. It was clear. No pirates to be seen. Which meant one thing.

He looked at the other officers and said, "Sit down on the floor with your backs against the bulkhead. Do it, now."

Then they waited.

Three black-clad pirates entered the bridge and stared at the officers seated on the floor. Not one of them had their faces covered, which didn't bode well. The big one, who'd fired at the bridge, grunted with satisfaction. He touched the throat mic and said, "Bridge is secure."

"All of you get up," he said, and the officers climbed to their feet. "Now, down into the hold."

––––––––

The small group shuffled inside and were told to stand against the rear bulkhead. The big pirate turned to another who had just entered. "Do you have all that is required?"

"Yes, sir."

"Good. Set the charges for ten minutes."

"Yes, sir."

Moreno felt his heart start to beat faster. Explosives! They were going to be killed. He came to his feet. "No! You cannot do it."

"Sit down," the big pirate snapped.

"No. I will not. You are going to kill us all."

"Last chance."

"No."

Then the pirate shot him.

In the leg.

Above the knee.

Moreno collapsed, clutching at his leg, crying out in pain.

The others, crew and officers, were startled by the sudden explosion, the noise reverberating around the confined space. Moreno rolled onto his side as though the position would help ease the pain.

The big pirate stepped forward, standing over the ship's captain. He pointed his weapon at Moreno and thought about what he would do. Then he lowered the gun. "It would be a waste of a bullet."

The big pirate turned away and walked towards the hatch, signaling to his men. Then the pirates left the hold and the door closed, leaving the ship's crew in the dark.

———

Cartagena, Spain, Present Day

It is said that all thieves end up in jail. This one was about to die. Casson Domingo had stolen from the wrong people this time, and they were hunting him relentlessly like a pack of starving dogs. From the heart of the Mediterranean to here in Cartagena. He wasn't sure how they had tracked him, yet here they were. Three men and a woman, all armed, determined to retrieve what he had taken.

Domingo patted his coat pocket as he stepped down to cross the street. Never would he have thought that something so small could have weighed so much. It was wrapped in cloth to keep it safe from damage.

His boots sounded loud on the damp street as he crossed it. Either side, tall sandstone façades reached up to the night sky, lit by sodium vapor lights.

Domingo glanced over his shoulder and saw the shadows emerge from an alley he'd just negotiated. His heart leaped. He was starting to wish that he'd never heard the tale of the treasure.

"You cannot escape us, Domingo," a woman's voice called out. "We will find you wherever you are."

Ahead of him a streetlamp lit a new intersection. He sped up, his lungs bursting from the exertion of his plight. He turned right, almost walking into a young couple heading in the opposite direction.

For the first time, as he looked ahead, Domingo smiled. People. Everywhere. He hurried forward into the crowd. The Cartagena Carnival was in full swing and young people from across Europe had come to party.

———

The four pursuers stopped at the intersection and stared at the dancing crowd before them. Carmen muttered a curse under her breath. They'd followed the thief this far and she wasn't about to lose him. "Spread out."

The three men with her did as she ordered, melting slowly into the crowd. All four were dressed in long coats down to their knees, hiding their weapons beneath them.

"Raven, do you see him?" Carmen asked.

A voice came through the earwig. "He is thirty feet ahead of your position, Carmen, and moving away."

"Thank you. Do not lose him."

"It is hard to keep track of him in the crowd."

"Do not…lose him."

Carmen stepped forward into the crowd, pushing her way between tightly packed revelers. Every so often one would bump into her, look into her emerald eyes, apologize, then keep partying.

"Carmen, he is still around thirty feet ahead of you."

She pressed on jostling with more revelers.

"He's getting away from you, Carmen. He's sped up. Now forty feet."

Carmen was becoming frustrated. "Cosimo, can you see him?"

"No."

"Luca, Marco. Can you?"

"Negative."

"Fifty feet."

Carmen increased her pace, this time not worrying about those around her. Using her shoulder, the red head knocked others out of her way. her athletic frame moving swiftly between revelers. One of those affected grabbed her by the shoulder, looking into her freckled face, and yelled, "Hey!"

Carmen turned and hit the young man in the throat, causing him to gag and sink to his knees. The girl with him shouted something and dropped down beside her friend, comforting him.

"Where is he?"

"I've lost him ahead of you."

"Find him." Her voice was businesslike yet held an undercurrent of menace.

"I'm trying."

"Christ," Carmen hissed and swept back her coat flap to reveal a Heckler & Koch MP7. It was hanging by a strap for easy access. She raised it above her head and opened fire into the air.

People scattered or dropped to the ground in panic.

Carmen scanned the chaos looking for their target. Then she saw him.

She pulled the stock on the MP7 and raised it to her shoulder. As she sighted, people flicked across her path, blocking the shot. Carmen grunted and squeezed the trigger, putting two revelers down with the long burst.

Cries of alarm and terror echoed as she tried to get a bead on Domingo. "Where is he?" she hissed.

"Ahead, to the left. He's panicking."

Carmen saw him and changed her aim. Once again, she fired and saw Domingo fall. She grunted with pleasure and strode purposefully forward. Already there were sirens sounding in the distance.

Carmen found Domingo where he'd fallen. He was gasping for breath, his lungs rapidly filling with blood from his wounds. She leaned down and went through his pockets. Restrained at first, but when she found nothing, her search became more urgent. But there was nothing.

The woman straightened, looking around. "He doesn't have it."

"Impossible," the voice in her earwig said. "We followed his progress all the way."

"I'm telling you it's not here," Carmen said bitterly. She grabbed Domingo by the shirt collar. "Where is it, thief?"

His mouth opened and closed as he struggled for breath.

Carmen growled a guttural sound and dropped him back to the pavement, looking around as though what she was seeking would suddenly appear. Marco appeared beside her, a big man with a dark beard, and like herself, with military experience. "We have to go, Carmen. Now."

The retrieval team leader nodded. "Shit."

1

THE CROSS

Everyone was gathered in the conference room of the Schmidt Foundation in Berlin, awaiting the appearance of the man himself, Johann Schmidt, founder, and CEO. The following day they were due to fly out to Portugal, but today, Schmidt was going to brief them on their new mission.

The building itself had once been a World War Two Flak Tower, now converted to serve a new purpose. Mark Butler sat in a stiff wooden chair flicking through his phone, a bored expression on his face. He was the newest addition to the Schmidt Foundation team, joining after his father had been murdered by a Neo-Nazi organization who, like the Schmidt foundation, had an interest in the lost treasures of the modern and ancient worlds. However, while Kurt Stuber was all about himself and power, Johann Schmidt sought to return all he could find to its rightful place.

Mark, in his mid-twenties, was dark-haired, and solidly built. He had been a soldier in a previous life before getting out.

"That looks interesting, handsome," a voice said from beside him.

A chair slid out and Molly Roberts, the foundation's electronic researcher sat down beside him. She was a Brit and known for speaking her mind. He looked at her and noted her hair. "Change of color, old girl?"

She grinned. Her hair had been pink the previous evening; now it was purple. "Like it?"

Mark nodded. "Actually I do. It makes you look like a grape."

She poked out her tongue and then grinned.

Mark said, "Now, tell me, what are we doing in Portugal?"

She leaned over and whispered softly in his ear, "You'll have to wait."

It was Mark's turn to smile. "Okay."

"Where's your fearless leader?" Molly asked, referring to Brooke Reynolds, the Foundation's head of security.

"Possibly doing her hair."

Molly rolled her eyes. "Uh, huh."

"What are you two talking about?" Isabella Pavesi asked from across the table. She was the Foundation's artwork and artifact expert. Mark thought of her as a pretty walking library. What was stored in her mind to do with her work was amazing. She was Italian, early twenties with fine features.

"We were talking about you," Molly said teasingly.

Isabella pulled a face and said jokingly, "I hope you bite your tongue."

Next to her sat Werner Krause, a German in his late twenties. Thickset, he was also the Foundation's historian. It was a toss up between him and their computer tech, Mr. Webster, who was the surliest.

Mark looked at Krause who scowled back. "Having a good morning, Werner?"

He grunted. "If you say so."

"Oh, come on, Werner, cheer up," Molly said to him. "Don't be so gloomy."

"Tell that to Greg," he growled.

"Wow, Werner, how to put a damn dampener on things," Mark growled.

The Greg he referred to was Greg Turow. He had been the team's leader of sorts, as well as their document investigator. He'd been killed when they were investigating stolen Nazi treasure. Kurt Stuber had had his claws into him after kidnapping his family, leveraging him to pass on information. The family had been rescued but Greg had died in an old salt mine in Austria. A bomb had been detonated in it, flooding its entirety. Mark and Brooke had been lucky to escape with their lives.

"Traitor got what was coming to him," Mr. Webster said.

Mark glared at the tech. He was the youngest of them all. Definitely him. "You're a happy custard."

A door opened and Schmidt entered the room followed by Brooke Reynolds. Brooke was the team's security chief. In her early thirties, she had an athletic build, stood about six-two, and had long dark hair. She had been a former member of the global phenomenon known as Team Reaper before getting out and following a passion: artifacts and treasures.

Schmidt on the other hand had gray hair, lined face, wore a suit and was a very rich man. Billionaire rich. The foundation was his idea, his baby as one would call it. Over the years he'd discovered countless artifacts and returned them to their rightful place. In all those years, he had been fortunate to never lose anyone who worked for him. Now in a very short space of time, he'd lost two.

Brooke took a seat next to Mark. He leaned over and said, "Was starting to think you weren't coming."

"I've been busy," she replied out of the corner of her mouth.

All eyes concentrated on the foundation's leader. Opening a folder he'd brought with him, he nodded at Molly who, using a small remote sequestered in her fist, turned on a large screen on the back wall.

A picture of a Spanish galleon appeared. Schmidt cleared his throat and said in his heavily-accented German voice, "Would anyone care to hazard a guess what we're looking at?"

"A Spanish galleon," Isabella suggested.

The billionaire nodded. "That's right. But which one?"

"The *Golden Hawk*," Krause supplied.

"Very good, Mr. Krause. The *Golden Hawk*. Anything to add, Mr. Krause?"

Krause sighed. "The *Golden Hawk* left the Caribbean in late sixteen-seventy-one. December, I think it was. It was under the escort of two smaller galleons commanded by Captain Esteban Ortega and Captain Cornelio Morales. All three ships disappeared. According to a lone survivor picked up by a passing galleon, there was a fight between Ortega and Morales which was instigated by Ortega. Morales's galleon was sunk, and Ortega was last seen disappearing into the fog looking for the *Golden Hawk*. None of them were seen again. The *Hawk* was commanded by Captain Alejandro Garza. With him was Bishop Hector Torres. From what I've read in the pages of history, Torres was a nasty human being."

"What was the ship carrying?" Mark asked.

"Gold and silver coins, jewels, tapestries, rings, fine plates, gold and silver ingots, jewel encrusted items," Isabella said. "Worth hundreds of millions in today's currency."

"And how does all this concern us?" Mark asked.

Schmidt took up the story again. "A few days ago, a cross appeared. A woman found it in her handbag. She thought it looked too valuable to keep so she took it to a museum in Madrid. After further examination it was found to be La Cruz de San Martín. The Cross of St. Martin. Isabella?"

"Really?" Isabella blurted. Her excitement skyrocketed.

Schmidt smiled at her enthusiasm. "Yes, really."

"Wow. The Cross of St. Martin was part of the Bishop's Treasure. It was discovered in Vera Cruz and thought to have been made by the Aztecs. We only have descriptions to go by but apparently that is where it came from."

"How did the cross end up in her handbag?" Mark asked.

Brooke said, "The other day, Cartagena, in Spain was celebrating one of their days by holding a carnival. While this was happening, four armed shooters appeared. Witnesses say they were chasing a man. One of the shooters opened fire in the crowd, killing some of the revelers. One of them was this man."

The picture changed. "Casson Domingo. Mr. Webster did some background on him, and he comes up as a petty thief. A burglar."

"Looks like he stole from the wrong person," Mark said, a low chuckle in his throat.

"From what can be pieced together, I would say that he was the one who stole the cross and these shooters were sent to get it back." The picture changed to show a grainy picture of the four shooters. "These are the ones responsible."

"Lot of firepower they're packing," Mark said.

"I'm thinking they'll be packing more than that,"

Brooke said. "Whoever these people are they have backing."

"Stuber?" Krause asked.

"No, not him. These people operate differently. They're doing it right out there in the open. It's like a warning. Our friend Stuber lurks in the shadows."

Mark nodded. "I agree with Brooke. These are cold killers."

"And they have the treasure," Isabella said.

Schmidt nodded. "It's possible, yes. Or this might be a one off."

"If this happened in Cartagena, then why are we going to Portugal?" Mark asked.

"Emilio Carris. He's a history professor in Sines, Portugal. He's been trying to find the *Golden Hawk* for years. Now it is our turn. Mr. Webster, see if you can find anything on the murderers. Molly, I want you to find out where our dead friend had been lately."

"Yes, sir."

"Let's get to it. We leave tomorrow."

———

The man stared at Carmen, displeasure etched in his face. Not only had she and her team failed to bring the cross back, it was now out in the open, and interest and excitement around the artifact was growing. Especially now that an organization called the Schmidt Foundation was involved.

"I am disappointed, Carmen," the man said. "You assured me you would get it back."

She nodded solemnly. "I am sorry, Excellency. I will take my team and retrieve it for you."

The man shook his head. "No. I have another job for you and your people."

"Doing what, Excellency?"

"All in good time, my dear. Come, sit at my feet, I have things to ask you."

"Yes, father."

"It does my heart good to hear you call me that."

Carmen sat down. "What is it you wish to know, father?"

"I am thinking of expanding our—my corporation."

"Yes, father. Where?"

"The Philippines."

"I see."

"Who would you recommend to take the helm?" the man asked his daughter.

"Jaco." Her answer was firm. "He knows what he is doing."

"You really think he is up to it?"

"He could do everything given half the chance," Carmen replied.

"That was what I thought too," the man replied. "So…"

"He would be a good choice."

The man nodded. "Tomorrow, you and your people will go to Portugal. I shall supply all the details before you leave. There is something you need to take care of."

A door opened and a man entered, a plastic container in his arms.

"What is Olavo doing here?" Carmen asked.

"I had him bring you a present."

The large man sat the plastic box on the floor near Carmen. She looked at it and then to her father, questioningly. He smiled; his anger seemingly gone. "Go ahead, open it."

She reached over and removed the lid before recoiling back violently, sliding on her buttocks across the marble floor. She looked at her father in horror. "What did you do?"

"It is just a reminder that I do not like failure. Even from you."

"But Luca? He did nothing wrong."

"He was with you; that was enough."

Carmen pointed at the container. "But, h—his head. He was my friend."

"And now he is dead. You may leave me now."

Carmen got to her feet.

"Take your friend with you."

Carmen's face screwed up in anger. "Get your lap dog to do it."

2

AIRCRAFT DOWN!

The Cessna Citation Longitude bounced as it hit turbulence flying over the Pyrenees. Mark looked over at Brooke, who sensed his eyes and glanced up from the book she was reading. "What is it?"

"I don't like it."

"Don't like what?"

"I've been thinking about the people who murdered the thief."

"And?"

"They're trained and have hi-tech capabilities. They don't care about who they have to kill to get what they want."

"And? Come on, Mark, get to the point."

"If we go upsetting them, they're going to come after us."

Brooke made big eyes at him. "Are you scared, Mark?"

He shook his head. "No, just worried about the others. You and I can take care of ourselves. Them, on the other hand, have all the fighting capabilities of a limp lettuce leaf."

"I heard that," Molly said, sitting up in her seat and turning it around.

"It wasn't an insult, just stating how things are," Mark said.

"I agree, if it came to a fight, we'd make Jerry Lewis look bloody good."

"What do you suggest, Mark?" Brooke asked, raising an enquiring eyebrow.

"What about a permanent security force when we're out in the field?" Mark asked.

Brooke looked thoughtful. "It might be worth a look. I'll mention it to Johann."

"Mention what to Johann?" Schmidt asked from where he was standing in the aisle.

"About a permanent security force to watch over you and the others."

He nodded. "I don't see why not."

"That's interesting," Molly said out loud to herself.

"What is?"

She spun her seat and they saw the laptop sitting on her knees. "I finally tracked our dead friend's movements. His last stop before Spain was Sicily."

"See if you can find out where."

"Yes, sir."

Isabella appeared. She was about to speak when the plane lurched with a pocket of turbulence. Schmidt said, "Everyone take a seat."

Mark looked at Isabella who had hold of a sheet of paper. "You look like someone who has something to tell."

"More like show," she said with a smile. "Here."

She passed him the piece of paper. It was a picture— of a cross. "Is this the one they found?"

"Yes."

"It looks plain but valuable. Something like the Aztecs would make."

She passed over a second piece of paper. "This is what it was thought to look like."

Mark nodded and passed both papers to Brooke. "They look the same," she said.

"I know. Maybe if we can trace it to the source, then we might find more."

"You're forgetting one thing, my pretty Italian friend," Mark said.

"Which is?"

"That source might have big guns and be willing to shoot anyone who comes looking."

"That's why we have you, handsome." A wry grin spread across her face.

Mark smiled back. "I knew it wasn't for my looks."

"Where did you get this sketch from, Bella?" Brooke asked.

"From the professor. He emailed me a copy."

Mark nodded and turned, looking out the window. It was a cloudless day and the sun shone brightly, even reflecting off—

"Holy shit!" he exclaimed when he saw the con trail. "Everyone get in your seats and strap in. Now!"

He glanced out the window and saw the trail getting closer. Beside him, Brooke asked, "What's the matter?"

"Someone just fired a fucking missile at us."

―――――

"Everyone hang on!" Brooke shouted.

Mark looked out the window. Impact was imminent and there was nothing they could do about it. He could only hope the end came quickly.

When it did come, however, it wasn't like he figured.

The explosion was loud, the plane lurched violently, and a hole opened in the starboard side, big enough to suck a human out as the Cessna depressurized.

Oxygen masks dropped from the ceiling and Mark struggled to grab one. He managed to get it to his face and then lost it as the plane dropped and rolled.

Somewhere in the cabin he heard one of the girls scream. He looked beside him and saw Brooke trying to get her own oxygen mask on.

Once more, Mark fumbled with his. It wasn't cooperating, but he eventually managed to place it over his nose and mouth. Glancing out through the window he saw the engine on fire. They were descending at a rapid rate.

Mark felt the blood rush to his head and his eyes started to flash. He felt himself becoming lightheaded. Beginning to fade into darkness. He shook his head to get rid of the cobwebs and looked around at the others. There were panicked expressions on their faces, but there was nothing he could do.

Then, ever so slowly, his eyes started to close as darkness overwhelmed him.

———

Pain. It was all he could feel as he started to come back to the here and now. Mark moaned and slowly opened his eyes. The sun stabbed at them. To his right was a large hole in the plane's fuselage. He looked out and saw that they were on the ground. He saw bits of debris, but somehow, the pilots had managed to get the plane down.

Mark looked around him and saw that everyone was still strapped in their seats, unconscious. At the rear of the plane was a large hole where the tail used to be. It had been ripped off when the plane had crashed landed.

Somehow, from where he sat, the front of the plane seemed to be intact.

A moan from beside him made him glance round and he saw Brooke's eyes flutter open. "Hey, are you OK?"

She looked at him, confused. There was blood on her arm, but it only looked to be superficial. "What happened?"

"We got shot down by a missile. Don't you remember?"

She frowned and looked at her surroundings. "We need to get out of here."

Mark nodded. "My thoughts exactly."

They removed their seatbelts and began checking the others one by one, waking them up. Amazingly, all had survived; a little banged up, but alive. They helped each other out through the tail of the plane and once outside, Mark could see the total devastation of what had happened.

Somehow the pilots had managed to get the plane down in the only open piece of land surrounded by trees. A great scar had been furrowed into the earth and a trail of debris left a telltale sign of their passage. Back there, Mark could see both wings and the tail section. He looked back at the fuselage of the plane and asked out loud, "How the hell did we survive that?"

"Are you OK?" Brooke asked him. "You look like you have a bump on your head."

Mark reached up and touched his forehead. He winced at the pain. "Never really noticed it. I guess I feel OK. What about you?"

"I feel like I've been run over by a steamroller," Brooke answered.

Mark nodded. "There is that."

Brooke looked around at the others who were seated

on the ground. "I'm going to check on the pilots if you want to check on these guys."

"Just be careful."

"I'm always careful. You know me."

"Yes, I do."

Brooke walked slowly around to the front of the plane to where the nose and cockpit should have been. Except it wasn't. The entire section was gone, back to the cockpit door. Along with the pilots.

"Oh, god no." She had known them both personally. Kent Taylor was married with two children. Helga Schultz, the only daughter of farmers outside of Hamburg. Now they were gone, their last act of bravery, getting the plane down to save their passengers.

She went back to the others. Johann Schmidt sat against a rock, stunned by what he was seeing before him. He saw Brooke and waved her over. "Are you all right, my dear?"

"I'm fine, Johann, just sore. You?"

He was cradling an arm. "I think there is something wrong with my shoulder."

"Let me look at it."

After a few moments she concluded, "I think you have a busted collarbone. Nothing too serious."

"Tell that to my arm."

"I need to find the sat phone to call for help."

Schmidt nodded. "It will be in the plane."

"I'll check."

She stood up, her body protesting as the adrenaline began to ebb, and pockets of pain set in. Before she could go back into the wreckage, Mark came back to her. "Did you find the pilots?"

"They're gone. The whole cockpit is gone."

"Shit."

"How are the others?" Brooke asked.

His face turned grim. "Molly is OK, a little banged up. Isabella has a concussion, Webster's leg's not good. It could be broken, and Werner. I think he's got a busted arm. How's Johann?"

"His collarbone is broken. We need to get them medical attention. I'm just going back in to see if I can find the sat phone."

"There is also one thing else you might want to consider," Mark said. "Whoever fired that missile could still be out there. We need our weapons."

"I'll see what I can find," Brooke replied. "In the meantime, keep a lookout."

Brooke returned to the interior of the plane's fuselage. It wasn't until she was in there that she totally realized how lucky they had been. By rights, they should all be dead.

Five minutes of searching revealed the sat phone and nothing else. Checking the phone she found that it wasn't working and threw it on the floor in a fit of temper. Only to pick it up again deciding that one of the others might be able to do something with it. She came back out and found Mark talking to Johann.

"The sat phone is stuffed. As for weapons," she waved at the debris field. "They're out here somewhere."

Mark nodded. "I'll have a look around."

Brooke sighed. "I'll see if one of the others can get this phone working."

————

The team sent to intercept the flight were, right at that moment, observing the crash site from the seclusion of the forest at the crest of a low ridge. There were six in total, all professionally trained and capable.

And armed to the teeth.

"There are survivors," said the man with the binoculars. "We must finish them off."

A second man nodded. "It will be easy. They are only treasure hunters."

"Let us hope so. Gather the men. We need to get it done before anyone comes looking. The alarm will have already been raised when the plane disappeared from radar. If we fail, I do not want to be the one to tell Carmen."

"I wouldn't want to be the one to tell her father."

The small team made their way off the ridge, picking their way through the rocks and trees. Their mission had been to shoot the plane down so that all on board would die. The first part of the task had been completed; not the second.

No one could be left alive.

———

Mark dropped the weapons bag on the ground. "This is all I could find."

Johann frowned and said between waves of pain, "Are you sure you will need them?"

Brooke nodded. "Yes, especially if those that shot us down are still out there."

"Do you think they are?"

"Possibly," Mark said taking out a Heckler and Koch P30 handgun followed by a Heckler and Koch G36. "Which one do you want?"

Brooke nodded at the P30. "Give me that one."

Mark tossed it to her, following up with some spare magazines. He dug around once more into the bag looking for spare mags for the G36. He found four and loaded one into the weapon, stuffing the rest into his pockets. "We don't have any body armor, but oh, well, can't live forever."

"Aren't you just full of cheer?" Brooke growled.

Mark grinned. "I thought I was being optimistic. I—"

"Shut up," Brooke hissed.

"What is it?"

"Listen."

Mark remained silent as he strained to discern what Brooke was hearing. Then he realized there was no noise at all. "We've got visitors."

"Yes, we have." Then she shouted, *"Everyone get under cover now!"*

No sooner had the words escaped her mouth than the whole crash site was lit up with gunfire.

———

Everyone took cover where they could, pinned down by the amount of gunfire. Brooke's warning had saved their lives. The incoming fire was coming from the tree line to their north.

"Christ," Mark growled and started to return fire with the G36. His rounds disappeared into the trees, and he was unable to tell if he'd hit anything.

Not far away, Brooke was cutting loose with the P30. Bullets peppered her position, forcing her to duck down. Mark called out, "I can't see them."

"Join the club. If we keep this up, we'll be out of ammunition and in deeper shit than we are now."

"Do you think you can circle around them if I give you some covering fire?"

"Can't be any worse than here."

Mark flicked the fire selector from semi to full auto and called across to Brooke. "Go!"

As soon as he opened fire, she was up and running, head down, but making good pace.

Bullets kicked up at her heels, but the shooters were too late. The trees ahead of her loomed up and she disappeared within.

Mark sank back down and changed the fire selector back to semi. His hope now was that Brooke could come through; otherwise they would all be dead.

———

Brooke dropped to a knee and placed her left shoulder against the trunk of a large conifer, its rough bark penetrating the thin fabric of her shirt. She paused a moment, letting her lungs capture all the breath they could.

The air in the forest smelled of pine sap and damp. She could feel the moisture in the soil soaking through the material of her pants.

Raising the P30, Brooke came up and began moving in the direction of the gunfire. She weaved between the trees until movement made her duck behind a tall trunk.

Two shooters were coming towards her, their weapons raised, sweeping left and right. They were obviously searching for her, but, as yet, hadn't seen any sign.

Brooke controlled her breathing, trying to get her heart rate to come down even further. The shooters came closer, slowly, deliberately. She listened for their footfalls. Then one of them trod on a stick which cracked, giving away their position.

Brooke came clear of the tree, her P30 raised and ready to fire. She squeezed the trigger once, changed her aim, and then squeezed it again. Both searchers' heads snapped back as the bullets penetrated their skulls. They dropped to the damp earth, their weapons spilling from their grasp.

Hurrying forward, Brooke knelt beside one of them, picking up a dropped weapon. It was a Beretta ARX160 assault rifle favored by the Italian armed forces. She grabbed some spare magazines, then came back to her feet, moving forward through the trees.

The shooting grew louder as she drew nearer, and she was suddenly upon their position; four men firing their weapons with furious disdain at those taking shelter below.

Inhaling a deep breath, Brooke brought the 160 up to her shoulder, and stepped out into the open.

Brooke squeezed the trigger and the 160 kicked back against her shoulder. The first shooter fell, a bullet in the side of his head. She changed her aim. Only to see that the three other shooters were already reacting. She fired once more. This time, bullets slammed into the chest of the second shooter. The rounds hammered into his chest armor and knocked him back. He was down, but not dead.

And the 160 shifted. This time she flicked the fire selector around to auto. She squeezed the trigger and the rifle rattled to life. The two stunned figures before her took multiple rounds each. They fell to the ground.

Before moving forward, she called out, "Cease fire. Cease fire."

Mark's firing stopped and an eerie silence settled over the forest. Two of the three men she'd just put down were only wounded. The third, the one who'd taken the round to his body armor in the chest, was stunned but still breathing. Brooke stamped on his chest with a boot, leaving it there, pointing the rifle at his head. The shooter moaned. His eyes opened and he looked up at her as she said, "Make one move and I'll put a fucking bullet in your brain."

Mark peered through the trees. "Looks like you've got this all wrapped up."

"Find something to tie these bastards up with."

Mark checked them and found some zippy ties he could use to fix their wrists together. With that done, he dragged the two wounded shooters over to where the other sat.

"Who are you?" Brooke asked.

They remained silent.

The sleeve on one of the wounded men's shirts had ridden up, exposing his forearm. There was a tattoo on it; two crossed cutlasses. "What do we have here?"

Mark took his cell out of his pocket and snapped a photo. "That could come in handy later."

"They're not going to speak," Brooke said.

"Then, let's see if what they have in their pockets does it for them."

"They have nothing on them," Brooke said. "It's like they sanitized themselves beforehand."

"Someone doesn't want us knowing who they are," Mark said. "Real professional operation."

"I know one thing," Brooke replied. "They are not Stuber's men."

"Which begs the question: who the hell are they?"

"Get some photos of their faces. Maybe we can get something through facial recognition."

"I have another question. Why would they want to shoot our plane down?"

"I don't know, Mark. I really don't know."

3

THE SPANISH ORDER

Their group was taken to a medical facility in Lleida, Spain where they could be patched up. The men who had attacked them had been taken away for questioning by the Spanish authorities.

The police had detained Mark and Brooke, interrogating them for an hour inside a local police station constructed of rendered brick. The exterior was painted blue and white, a large sign showing a crest with Policia written underneath it.

It was sometime later before two Interpol officers appeared, taking over the investigation. Katja Janssen and Ruben Bakker were both well dressed and focused on their work.

"Do you have any idea who these people are?" Janssen asked.

"No," replied Mark. "They're new to me."

She looked questioningly at Brooke. "Search me. Don't you know?"

Their investigations had turned up nothing. Janssen shook her head. "I'm afraid not. Do you know why anyone would want to shoot your plane down?"

Mark gave them a thoughtful look. "Hmm. I think I know. They were trying to kill us."

Brooke glared at him. "Not helping, Mark."

"Sorry, dumb damn question."

"Why were you going to Portugal?" Bakker asked.

"Why don't you ask Johann? He'll tell you what you need to know," Brooke said.

"He is asleep."

She nodded. "We're treasure hunters. We seek out relics, artifacts, and stuff like that and return them to their rightful owners."

"So your trip to Portugal is to do with…treasure hunting?" Bakker suggested.

"That's right."

He looked skeptical. "I see."

Mark bristled. "What is that supposed to mean?"

"Nothing. It's just I wouldn't picture people such as yourselves as treasure hunters."

"What type do you figure?" Mark asked.

"Maybe a little more eccentric," Bakker replied.

"You mean crazy."

The man smirked. "I did not say that."

"You meant it."

"You act more like mercenaries."

"We cannot help it if people try to kill us," Brooke shot back at him.

"All right, enough." Janssen said. "Shall we get back to what we are doing?"

"My thoughts exactly," Brooke agreed.

"Is there anyone you can think of making threats against you lately?" Janssen asked.

Brooke's thoughts went to Stuber. "How long do you have?"

"As long as it takes."

"I'm glad I was asleep." Schmidt said. "I'm too tired to take such a—how do you say—grilling?"

"Something like that," Brooke said.

"Where is Mark?"

"I think he and Molly are with Isabella. Who knows what they're up to?"

"How are the others?"

"Fine. Webster has a broken leg and Werner a broken arm. Nothing a little rest won't hurt. Webster is trying to run down a few things for us."

Schmidt nodded. "He never stops, that boy."

"No. He may be a pain in the ass, but he's good at what he does."

Someone cleared their throat from the doorway. Expecting it to be a nurse they both looked around to see a woman with collar length dark hair, wearing glasses, dressed in a knee-length blue dress. Schmidt frowned. "May we help you?"

"I hope so," the woman said with an Australian accent. "I'm Grace Cramer, your new document investigator."

Schmidt stared at Brooke. "Sorry, Johann, I forgot to tell you, I hired somebody else. Not the one you wanted."

Grace entered the room. "I'm sorry—"

"No, don't be," Schmidt said. "I'm sure it's just an oversight."

Brooke stepped forward. "I'm Brooke Reynolds, this is Johann Schmidt. We're pleased to meet you."

"Likewise."

Brooke turned back to her boss. "Grace is Australian. She used to work for ASIO, Australian Intelligence. I convinced her to come and work for us."

"What was wrong with the other applicant?" Schmidt asked.

"Grace has firearms training and field experience."

Grace said, "Look, if you don't want me, I can go back to Australia. I might need to find a different job, but—"

"No, we want you," Brooke said. "Don't we, Johann?"

He nodded. "Trial basis. Your starting salary will be two hundred thousand US. If you meet the mark, then it will double."

Grace was stunned. "Wow, that much?"

"If it isn't enough, I'm sure we can come to some other arrangement."

"Oh, no. No, no, no. That is more than sufficient. I'd settle for the starting rate."

"That won't be necessary," Schmidt said curtly.

"When would you like me to start?"

"Now. Brooke will tell you your duties."

Brooke escorted her out into the hallway. "I'm sorry, Grace, he's in pain and a little testy. The whole mix-up thing is my fault too."

"That's all right." She hesitated. "I got your message and redirected. But just out of curiosity, how did you all end up here?"

"Our plane was shot down by a missile."

Grace smiled then realized that Brooke was actually serious. "Oh, dear."

"Yes, there's no shortage of action here. As for what you'll be doing, I'll fill you in as you meet the rest of the team."

"Great."

"I'm not sure you'll think that once we're done."

———

"And lastly, we have Mark Butler. He's a jack of all trades around here."

Mark took Grace's hand. "Ma'am."

"Mark."

"Glad to have you aboard."

"I'm glad to be here."

"Are you a real spook?" Molly asked.

"I suppose I was."

"Good, because you'll know shit and be able to teach me all the good stuff."

Grace grinned. "Such as?"

"Such as how not to hack into places you're not meant to be," Brooke growled.

"Do you know much about artifacts and things?" Isabella asked.

"Not a lot, but I'm good with documents."

"I will teach you."

"I look forward to it."

"Clear the way, coming through," Webster called out as he whirled into the room in a wheelchair, his broken left leg elevated.

Brooke rolled her eyes as he stopped just shy of Mark. He looked at him and said, "Move."

Mark stood there. "How would you like me to break your other leg, Webster?"

The tech glared at him. He opened his mouth and said, "That's Mr. Webster."

Brooke looked at Grace. "We're just one big happy family."

"So I see."

"I have something if you want it?" Webster said.

That got their attention. "What?" Brooke asked.

"Those photos that Jeeves took—"

"Jeeves?" Brooke asked.

"Butler, Jeeves."

"Shit. Keep going."

"Anyway, they're all dead."

Mark stared at Webster. "Actually, if you are referring to P.G. Wodehouse, Jeeves was a valet, not a butler. Now, elaborate."

"Every one of those men whoever they are, are dead. Have been for at least two years. Some longer."

"The mystery deepens," Mark said. "Anything else?"

"The tattoo. They all had them. Not sure what the link is yet."

"Would you like some help?" Grace asked.

Webster stared at her. "Who are you?"

"Grace Cramer, the new document investigator and your boss."

"OK, I can live with that."

"Do you want my help or not?"

"What did you do before?"

"I worked for ASIO."

"All right, I'll let you help."

Grace stifled a grin. "Fine, let's get started."

She departed with Webster, leaving the others in the room. "I think she'll fit right in," Mark said.

"That's good because we still have to go to Portugal," Brooke said.

"In case you didn't realize, we were in a plane crash."

"They can return to Berlin and support us from there. We need to go talk to the professor."

"Fine, we'll do that."

"Good."

"When do we leave?"

"Just as soon as I talk to Johann."

————

"What happened?" Carmen asked Marco.

"I'm not sure," the big man with dark hair said. "The plane was shot down, but they all survived except for the pilots. Then on the ground somehow, they managed to take out the team. Three were killed, three were wounded and have been taken into custody by the Spanish police. They are soon to be handed over to Interpol."

"That can't happen. They need to be silenced before they can talk."

"They wouldn't talk," Marco said.

"We can't take that chance. My father would not be pleased."

"All right, I will have it taken care of."

"Thank you, Marco. Now, there is the other matter."

Marco nodded. "We have someone watching over him. What would you like done?"

"Keep the surveillance. If I guess right, they will still come. I want to know what they are up to."

"Not kill them like your father wished?" Marco asked apprehensively.

"I have a feeling it is not going to be that easy. But first, I want to know what they are up to and if they are a danger to everything. Then we will kill them."

———

Lleida, Spain

A four-vehicle convoy awaited the arrival of the three men who were escorted under armed guard to an armored truck. Three black SUVs made up the rest of the convoy. After being loaded, they were ready to be transported to Lyon in France.

Across the street, in a blue BMW, sat two men. Both wore casual clothes and dark sunglasses. As the small convoy pulled away, the man in the passenger seat said into his encrypted cell, "They are moving now."

"Follow them. Do not be seen."

Turning to his companion, the passenger said, "Follow them."

Allowing a few vehicles to pass before pulling into the line of traffic, they drove through the streets, remaining several cars behind the small convoy. As the miles rolled on, the traffic thinned, and when they eventually left the town, they dropped further back as they hit the open road. The passenger dialed the number again. "They are out of Lleida."

"Stop there."

As they pulled onto the verge, they lost sight of the convoy heading over a rise in the road. As they sat in their vehicle waiting for further instructions, an explosion rocked the Spanish countryside as an AGM (Air to Ground Missile) destroyed its target.

Sines, Portugal

The port city of Sines had a deep-rooted history, from the Punics, to Egyptians, and Romans. The latter, using the port as an industrial center. Then in the Middle Ages, Sines was occupied by the Visigoths and ransacked by Moors.

Now it held visitors enthralled by its picture-perfect scenery and vacation destination by the sea where everyone wanted to go. Narrow alleys with cobblestones, private balconies overlooking them, secluded beaches, specialty shops, and sparkling seas.

"I could live here," Mark commented as they drove along beside the harbor. "It's quite nice."

Brooke nodded. "It's OK I guess."

"You have somewhere else in mind?" Mark asked.

"Santorini."

"Start saving your cash, Brooke."

She smiled as she turned the Range Rover to the right. "I don't need to. I already have a place there."

"Bullshit."

"No bullshit. Johann pays well."

"You'll have to show me one day," he said.

"Maybe I will…when you grow up some."

Mark shook his head. "I can't believe it. Brooke Reynolds owns a place in Santorini. Do you have pictures?"

She nodded. "Back in Berlin."

"Well then, remind me to hit you up for a bo-peep."

"If you're lucky."

They continued along the cobbled streets, taking in more of the beauty of the small seaside city. Brooke slowed the SUV and pulled over to park. "Here we are."

As they looked at the small corner building before them, they saw the white walls with yellow trim, and low fence-type bars across double French doors which swung in and made it like a balcony.

"The professor sure has a nice place," Mark said. "And a view."

Alighting from the Range Rover, they closed the doors. Both had handguns tucked into their pants at the back in case anything untoward should happen, given the attempt on their lives by having been shot out of the sky.

Brooke knocked on the door and after a couple of minutes a middle-aged man with graying hair answered it. Brooke smiled. "Professor Emilio Carris?"

"Yes."

"I'm Brooke Reynolds. This is Mark Butler. Johann Schmidt sent us."

A look of relief came across his face. "Please, come in." His voice was heavily accented, but his English was good.

The pair were surprised to find the interior of the home incongruent with what they had seen outside. While the exterior held the charm and age of the city, inside was more modern with sparse furnishings and a tiled floor. Against the far wall were some shelves that held various artifacts.

It was a display that instantly drew Mark's attention, and he walked straight over to it.

There were gold coins, some broken pottery, a short piece of wood, and a chain with a cross on it. The cross was what caught Mark's attention. It was made of gold, inlaid with emeralds.

Carris said, "It is the cross, isn't it?"

Mark nodded, not taking his gaze from it. "It's beautiful."

"It was taken from the wreck of a Spanish Galleon which was discovered off Florida in the United States. I was part of the team that found it. Some of the other artifacts on the shelves were discovered with it."

"Was that the *St. Marie*?" Mark asked.

"Yes, it was."

"If I recall correctly, you lost a diver on that excursion."

Carris nodded. "It was not an easy dive. Currents, sharks, among other things. The diver we lost…" He paused, remembering. "Would you like a drink? Coffee?"

They both nodded. Brooke said, "That would be great, thank you."

The kitchen was open plan, so while he prepared the drinks, Carris was able to address them. "Johann called me and told me what had happened. A bad thing. I trust you are both fine—of course you are, you are here."

"It was a close-run thing," Mark replied.

"Who would do such a thing?"

"We have an idea who, but we're running searches to confirm it. A very specific tattoo on the attackers have presented a clue which is being followed up."

The professor put the cups on a small coffee table. "A tattoo? May I see it? That is, if you were able to get a picture."

"Sure," Mark replied, digging into a pocket for his cell. He punched in his code and brought up the picture, turning the phone around so the professor could see it.

Carris grunted and held up an index finger. "Yes. Wait here."

He went over to his table and slid it aside. Leaning down, he lifted a rug to reveal a square trapdoor in the floor, opening it with a creak, and removing a small diary, tattered from wear. He flicked through the pages until he settled on one then showed it to Mark. The small drawing was the same as the picture. Mark looked at him questioningly.

Carris nodded knowingly then showed the picture to Brooke. "It is the mark of the Spanish Order."

Brooke looked up. "The Spanish Order? Who are they?"

"Pirates."

"Really?"

"Yes. They can be traced back to the sixteenth century."

"And they are still around today?" Mark asked in astonishment.

Carris stared at them. "Haven't you just proven that?"

"You don't happen to know where they hang out, do you?"

Carris shook his head. "I'm sorry, no. But as you can see, they're not like the pirates of old."

Brooke said, "Can you tell us about the *Golden Hawk*?"

"Back in the late sixteen hundreds the ship disappeared along with its escort. The only survivor related the story of Captain Esteban Ortega attacking the galleon of his comrade Captain Cornelio Morales. Morales's ship was sunk, and Ortega went after the *Hawk*. They were never seen again."

"And you've been searching for the *Hawk*," Mark said.

"That's right," Carris said holding up his notebook. "It's all in here."

"What have you found out so far?" Brooke asked. "Anything that could help us?"

"Everything we have discovered has been from rumor or is a dead end," Carris explained.

"What kind of rumors?" Mark asked.

"That Ortega was of the Spanish Order, which makes sense if he attacked the galleon Morales commanded. Another rumor is that the *Hawk* was seen in the Med."

"Really?"

The professor nodded and opened his little book. "Here, I'll read you an excerpt from a diary I found."

"...and there coming out of the haze was a large ship in full sail. She had two rows of guns and looked a ghostly sight. But what made her stand out was the golden hawk on her bow, wings stretched as though she was flying. But a great cloud sailed with her and death a constant companion..."

Mark nodded. "What do you suppose that last piece meant?"

The professor shrugged. "I don't know. It could be anything."

"Where was she supposedly sighted?" Brooke asked.

Carris thought for a moment before opening his

mouth to speak but then paused again as an idea came to him and he looked urgently at his watch. "I'm sorry, I forgot I have to be at another appointment. Listen, why don't you come back tomorrow, and we'll go through some more of my diary? Maybe we might find something that you and Johann can use."

Brooke nodded. "Thank you, that would be great."

"Good. It is settled."

4

THE KILLER REDHEAD

Sines, Portugal

Brooke and Mark were hanging out in their large hotel room, sharing pizza, and talking to the rest of the team over a secure internet connection. The room was one of many in the 5-star hotel. Soft towels had been left on each bed, and the minibar was full. Their balcony overlooked a large pool. Upon checking into their room, when Mark had seen it, he'd said, "I'm not going out that way again."

"What do you have?" Schmidt asked from the laptop in front of the pair.

Brooke said, "Carris has a book—a diary—in which he keeps all his notes. We also found out a few interesting pieces of information. This first bit should help Grace and Webster. The Spanish Order. They were pirates in the sixteenth century. They are the ones who attacked us."

Grace's picture appeared on the screen. "That's great to know. We'll dig into it."

Brooke continued. "Werner, this one is for you. Apparently, the *Hawk* was sighted by someone in the Mediterranean sometime after its disappearance."

Krause appeared. "I'll look into it. It'll be a place to start."

"Do you have anything else?" Schmidt asked.

"No, not yet. We're going back tomorrow to have a look at Carris's diary to see what else we can learn."

"All right, keep me updated. And good luck."

"Thank you, sir."

The call ended and Mark tossed a half-eaten piece of pizza back into the box. "That's like eating cardboard. You want to go down to the restaurant for a decent meal?"

Brooke pulled a face and tossed down the slice she'd been eating. "I thought it was just me. You buy."

Mark grinned. "Just for you."

The pair grabbed their gear and room card and left the room, heading for the elevator. They caught it down to the right level, taking in the luxurious finishes of the wide, carpeted hallway as they strolled to the restaurant. A smiling maître d' met them at the entrance and showed them to a table for two. When they were seated and he'd placed napkins in their laps, he asked, "Would you perhaps like some champagne?"

Mark and Brooke looked at each other and Mark said, "Two beers will be fine."

"Yes, sir."

They sat and talked while waiting to order. Most of the discussion centered around their work. Eventually it came to Cramer. "How did you come to choose her?" Mark asked.

"I saw her when I was in Australia once. When I was working with Global. We liaised, not me personally, with ASIO on a drug ring we were running down. She was very good at what she did, and I knew if I could get her, she would fit right in."

"You think she'll work out?" He raised an enquiring eyebrow.

Brooke nodded. "I'm sure she will. Even better is that she can handle herself. Like having a permanent security officer around the team while we're away."

Eventually, they ordered their meals, Brooke choosing a fish and salad, and Mark had a beef concoction with gravy and vegetables. While they were eating, Brooke noticed that he kept looking over her shoulder. "What is it?"

He flicked his gaze to her and said, "I think we might have a dicker."

Brooke rolled her eyes. "Oh, God, not you."

Mark frowned. "Not me what?"

"Dicker. I used to work with a guy who used that term."

Mark nodded. "I picked it up while I was in Afghanistan from a Brit. It means—"

"I know what it means, Mark. Where is he?"

"Over your left shoulder two tables back. There are two of them. Both fighting-age males."

"You're not in the desert now, sunshine," Brooke reminded him.

"Sorry. The more I do this job, the more I feel like I'm back in the military." Mark thought for a moment. "Have you finished your meal?"

Brooke looked at him suspiciously. "Why?"

"I'll be right back."

Mark got up and walked towards the table where the two men sat. As he walked past, he pretended to stagger, then trip. Next thing he was sprawling across one of the men. The man reacted instantly by trying to shove Mark away. Apologizing profusely, Mark gained his feet and kept walking.

Brooke watched it all unfold then as Mark moved off,

he made eye contact with her. She dropped money on the table, came to her feet, and followed him out of the restaurant.

———

As they climbed into the elevator, a less than impressed Brooke asked, "What was all that?"

Mark lifted his shirt a touch to reveal a handgun; it looked to be a Taurus G3. Brooke rolled her eyes. "Shit, Mark."

"That's not all." He took a wallet out of his pocket and held it up with a smile. "I got this too."

Brooke reached out and took it. She was about to open it when the elevator dinged, and the door slid open to their floor. She stuffed it into her right rear jeans pocket and said, "Come on."

Back in the room she retrieved it and checked what was inside. What she found was some paper money, a little change, and some cards. The name on the driver's license was Paul Revere. "Not very original," she said showing Mark.

"Not at all."

"I'll take some pictures and send them through to Grace."

Mark examined the handgun. "Nice piece of equipment."

"You know they're going to come looking for these, don't you?"

"That's the plan. Maybe we might get some answers."

Ten minutes later, there was a knock at the door. "Room service."

Brooke and Mark stared at each other. It was a woman. Not what they were expecting. Mark shrugged and walked over to the door. He peered through the spy hole and saw a woman in her late twenties, with freckles and long red hair tied back in a ponytail, wearing a white house keeping jacket.

"We didn't order anything."

She held up a piece of paper and said, "I'm sorry, sir, but this is the room number I was given. If you could check the names on the paperwork?"

Mark glanced back at Brooke who had a weapon in her hand. She nodded and hid the handgun behind her back.

Cautiously Mark opened the door only to have it flung back into him by a swift kick from the opposite side. "Shit!" he exclaimed as he staggered back, kicking himself for his stupidity.

Carmen entered the room with a suppressed weapon in her right hand. Before she could fire, Mark gathered himself and swung the door back. It hit Carmen's arm, and when she fired her weapon, the bullet burned harmlessly into the wall.

With a growl of rage, she tried to correct her aim, but Mark hit her forearm and the weapon spilled from her grasp.

Undeterred, she came in closer and lashed out with a fist, catching Mark in the side of his head. He staggered back into the room proper, and Carmen followed him. Mark tried to retaliate with a punch of his own, but it was blocked, followed by a swift kick which caught him in the stomach, doubling him over.

Carmen glanced up and saw Brooke with her handgun pointed in her direction. She dived to the left and scooped up a vase of flowers just as Brooke fired. The bullet punched into the door behind Carmen, the discharge echoing loudly.

Drawing her arm back, Carmen hurled the vase at Brooke who managed to duck out of the projectile's way.

It missed but Carmen followed it up closely and threw herself at the Schmidt Foundation security expert. A shoulder caught Brooke in the middle, knocking the air from her lungs.

They crashed to the floor, Carmen on top. She hit Brooke twice, drawing blood from the corner of her mouth. "Fucking bitch," Carmen hissed and hit her again.

Her fist came back once more but the blow never landed because Mark crashed into her from the side, the pair sprawling across the floor.

A growl of frustration escaped Carmen's lips as she exploded into motion. An elbow came around and hit Mark in the stomach, causing his knees to jerk up.

The attacking woman came smoothly to her feet, crouched, her muscles bunched, ready to uncoil. She saw a handgun on the floor and went to dive on it, but Brooke hit her from the side, driving Carmen back into the wall.

Carmen brought her fists down onto Brooke's back, mustering all the power she could. Brooke grunted and staggered. Then she came up, bringing her knee into Carmen's middle.

Carmen doubled over, all the air in her lungs escaping through her mouth. She gasped and coughed, trying to suck in what had been expelled. Brooke hit her again, but Carmen stayed on her feet. Another blow followed, and Carmen sank to a knee.

Brooke moved in for the coup de grace and Carmen surprised her by spinning on her bent leg, sweeping Brooke's feet with the other.

"Fuck!" Brooke exclaimed as she fell hard to the floor.

Carmen rolled over and dropped an elbow into Brooke's stomach before coming back to her feet and removing the room attendant's jacket, revealing a black tank top.

Breathing hard, Carmen stepped towards Brooke, raising a boot to stomp down hard on her face.

"Hey, bitch!" Mark shouted from across the room. "I'm still in this damn fight."

"Not for fucking long," Carmen hissed and ran at him, covering the short distance in the blink of an eye.

She leaped, leaving the floor, and extending a leg out straight. It hit Mark in the chest, driving him back into the wall behind him. His head crashed into the drywall sending blinding flashes through his head and eyes. Mark dropped to his knees, stunned by the impact.

Carmen looked at the devastation around her. Both of her targets were now down. Spotting her weapon amongst the debris, she walked over to it. Panting hard, she stood for a moment to catch her breath before bending to pick up the weapon, her fingers wrapping around the grip. Then, as she started to straighten up, Brooke was there, coming from nowhere.

The Foundation member lashed out with a boot, catching Carmen in the ribs. Still clutching at her handgun, Carmen reeled away, a cry of pain exploding from her mouth. Her left shoulder hit the wall, keeping her upright but sending pain shooting through her body.

Then Brooke had her own weapon in her hand and like a scene in a long-forgotten action movie they started shooting at each other, missing with every shot while trying to avoid being hit themselves.

Screaming in pure frustration, Carmen shot the sliding glass door onto the balcony before running at the cascading glass.

Carmen exploded through the opening and launched herself over the balcony into the darkened abyss below.

Running to the rail, Brooke was just in time to see her attacker hit the water of the pool below. She stood there and watched as Carmen swam to the edge and climbed out, looked up, and then disappeared.

There was a moan behind Brooke, and she turned to see Mark lurching towards her.

"Oh, God," she groaned and hurried to help him. "Are you alright?"

"I feel like I've been worked over by a fucking tank."

"Me too. The bitch could fight." There was a grudging respect in Brooke's voice. "But that isn't our problem. Get your stuff, we need to get out of here."

"Don't we just."

———

Carmen clenched her jaw as Marco put another stitch in the flesh of her wounded shoulder, but she emitted no sound. As a little girl she'd been taught that crying was a sign of weakness. She never cried.

When he was finished, Marco put more iodine on the wound and then covered it. She nodded, her pride still hurting from the beating she'd received in the hotel. "Thank you, Marco."

Coming to her feet, Carmen walked across the room and out onto the balcony. The night air was cool against her skin, the moon shining onto the ocean which reflected its light. Her father was not going to be happy when he found out. All she could do now was regroup and try again.

There was movement behind her. Carmen turned to see Cosimo, the lithe, darkhaired assassin of her team. "There is an avenue we can still pursue, Princess."

Carmen flinched internally. She hated the title bestowed upon her. "Which one is that, Cosimo?"

"The professor."

He was right. The professor would be a good place to continue. She nodded. "Yes, let's go and see him."

Before they could leave, Carmen's cell buzzed. She knew who the caller was even without looking at the screen. "Father?"

"Yes, Princess, it is me."

Her face hardened. "Don't call me that."

"Why not? You are a princess after all."

"No, I'm not," she shot back at him, tired of his games.

"Tell me what happened," her father said. His voice now had an edge to it. He knew, somehow. He always knew.

"It is nothing. I'm rectifying the situation."

"Really? I have looked into these people myself, Carmen. From what I can tell they are very good at what they do. I want them dead before they mess everything up. If you can't see to it, then I will send Olvado to clean up your mess."

"Do not send your lap dog anywhere near me, father, or I will bury him."

His voice grew savage. "Watch your mouth, girl. Do not think that because you are my daughter that I would not punish you in our ways like I have done the others."

Carmen's jaw set firm. Her voice was bitter. He may have been her father, but she hated the man. "Yes, Your Grace."

"Now, what are you going to do about it?"

"I am going to see the professor, to ask him some questions."

He nodded. "Good. Do not leave him alive when you are finished."

"I did not intend to," Carmen replied.

"Is there anything you need, daughter?"

"Just one thing, father. Whoever you have following me around, I will find them, and send you their head."

Her father chuckled. "If you find them, my dear, I expect you to. But just so we are clear, I don't have anyone following you."

The call ended and she cursed silently. Her father was a dangerous man, but one day she would kill him, and then she would be free.

———

The third fingernail coming away from its root bed was what broke Professor Carris. The beating he'd weathered, the first two nails that hurt like hell, the pain eating into his brain. The third one, however, was the final straw.

"All right, I'll tell you!" he screeched as he strained against the ropes binding him to the chair.

Cosimo stopped what he was doing and stepped back. Carmen nodded with satisfaction and said, "Thank you for seeing things our way, Professor. Now, what did the people from the Schmidt Foundation want?"

"They were here about the *Golden Hawk*," Carris replied.

"What about it?"

"I guess they wanted information."

"What did you tell them?" Carmen asked.

"Not much. I had to go out, so they are coming back tomorrow."

"I asked you what, Professor?"

"That the ship was seen in the Mediterranean."

"What else?"

He stared at Carmen. There were tears in his eyes and wet streaks on his cheeks. His eyes shifted to her arm. "They asked about the tattoos. I see yours is different. Someone important, maybe?"

Carmen nodded. "Maybe."

"You are his daughter," Carris said.

Carmen was stunned by Carris's deduction. He could see it in her eyes and couldn't help but grin. His split lips bled some more. "You don't think after all these years I haven't heard the rumors? The Spanish Order led by one man. The difference in the tattoo tells me that you are special. That makes you his wife or daughter. I will say daughter."

"You do not know what you are talking about," Carmen hissed.

Carris nodded knowingly. "This close and now I am to die. But before you kill me, tell me your name. Tell me if I am right."

Carmen shook her head. "No."

And with that, Cosimo stepped in behind Carris and cut his throat.

———

As Brooke and Mark approached the door to Carris's home, they could see it was ajar ever so slightly, but seeing it raised the hair on Brook's neck, making her reach for the P30. It came free from her waistband, and she dropped it down to her side. Mark saw her move and did the same, his pains from the night before forgotten in an instant.

Mark's weapon came up without hesitation and he waited for Brooke to move. She glanced at him, and he nodded stoically. Easing the door open, she stepped across the threshold.

Mark followed her in and soon smelt the familiar coppery scent of blood. Training took over for them both as they cleared their way into the main open plan area where they found Carris still tied to the chair, his throat cut.

"Check the bedroom," Brooke said softly.

Mark did so and found it clear. He joined Brooke back with Carris. "Looks like they tortured him," she said.

Looking around the room, Mark had an epiphany and moved quickly over to the table and shoved it aside. He lifted the mat and then the trapdoor, looking inside. Carris's diary lay where the professor had placed it. "It's still here."

"Then they didn't know about it which means whoever did this was after something else."

Mark looked across at the display. Everything, including the cross and chain was still there. "The artifacts are still there, which means they were after information."

"Yes, but about what?"

"Or who?" Mark replied looking across at her.

Brooke nodded. "They were after information about us. It had to be the Spanish Order."

Mark flicked through the diary. "There's a lot here. We need to get it back to Berlin where it can be looked at properly."

Brooke said, "I agree. But we also need to do something about Carris."

The decision was taken out of their hands as distant sirens could be heard growing closer, louder. Mark looked at Brooke. "Do you get the feeling that they are coming for us?"

"I have no doubt. We've just been set up. Let's move."

Mark tucked the diary into his shirt, and they ran towards the front door. No sooner had they stepped outside when three police cars appeared. "Back inside!" Brooke exclaimed.

They turned and went back in, locking the door. Mark said, "That won't hold them for long. Let's try the back."

Running through the professor's home, the pair found the rear door. Mark opened it and caught sight of another police car on the street behind. "Shit. Back in."

There was a pounding on the door out front accompanied by shouts. Mark looked for a place to hide. "Christ, we're screwed."

Then he saw it. The trap into the ceiling. He dragged the table across beneath it and climbed up. He opened the trap and looked at Brooke. "Quick, up here."

She climbed up onto the table and he helped her up through the opening. Behind them he heard the door splinter. Mark grabbed the diary and forced it into Brooke's hand. "Go."

He jumped down and moved away from the table to await the police who were mere heartbeats away. Above, Brooke closed the trap and heard the shouting below as the first officers barged into the living room.

5

OLD FRIENDS, NEW ENEMIES

Sines, Portugal

The terracotta tile slid out with little effort followed by another. Soon Brooke had enough removed that she could climb from the cavity and onto the roof. Crouching, she crept forward to look down, seeing four police cars parked out the front on the street. She eased back and looked to her left where the orange roofline continued for hundreds of meters as the terrace buildings stretched into the distance.

Brooke knew that if she was to be any help to Mark, she had to get away. So, as silently as possible, she crept along the rooftop, trying not to dislodge any of the tiles in case they slid off and dropped onto the cobbled street below, giving her position away.

Once Brooke figured she had reached a safe distance from the crime scene, she dropped down to the street, staying on her haunches until—

"Everything is clear."

Brooke whirled around, her P30 up and pointed at the face of…Anika Meyer.

"Hello, Brooke," Anika said with a smile.

Anika Meyer, in her early thirties, the great grand-daughter of famous Nazi, Kurt 'Panzer' Meyer, was tall with dark hair cut into a bob. She wore jeans and a shirt that hung loose to cover the Glock handgun she had hidden. Brooke's weapon was unwavering. "What are you doing here?"

"Observing," she replied.

"Why?"

"Shall we go somewhere else and talk before the police come along?" Anika asked.

"I can't, I need to help Mark."

Anika shook her head. "You can't. Not yet. Come with me and I'll help you."

Brooke gave her a doubtful look. "You want me to trust you?"

"You have no one else." Meyer raised an eyebrow at Brooke.

Brooke knew she was right. "Why do you want to help me?"

"Let's just say that there is a mutual benefit for me helping you."

"You mean it benefits Stuber."

"Something like that. But you can't let the police get you. They are not who you think they are."

"What do you mean?" Brooke asked.

"They work for the Spanish Order."

"What about Mark?"

"We will wait until he is inside their jail and then we will get him back," Anika said.

"Who is this Spanish Order?" Brooke asked.

Anika grunted. "They are everywhere."

"You realize that if I agree, this doesn't change anything."

"I would not expect it to."

The police never questioned Mark, even after they arrived at the police station. He was shoved roughly into a cell and then left on his own. Which was odd because they had arrested him for murder. Or had they? He sat on the edge of a lumpy cot and waited patiently for two hours in the stuffy heat for someone to come and talk to him. But during that time, nobody came. He just sat there, mulling everything over in his mind. Then the door opened, and she appeared.

"Hello, Mr. Hunter," the woman said. "I'm glad we have this chance to talk."

It was the woman who had been in the hotel room trying to kill him and Brooke. "Who are you?" he asked.

"My name is Carmen," she supplied without hesitation, not caring that he knew.

"You were the woman at the hotel. You fight like a wildcat."

"I will take that as a compliment," Carmen replied. "You need to improve your skills."

Mark nodded. "I'm a little rusty."

"Oh, well, it won't matter now. Tell me, why are you here in Sines?"

Mark decided that she already knew so he might as well cut to the chase. "We're looking for the treasure of the *Golden Hawk*."

"I see."

"But you already had that figured out, which was why you had our plane shot down. Shame about your people."

Her expression didn't change. "Plenty more fish in the sea."

"Or pirates on it," Mark replied.

Carmen nodded. "That too."

"But you're not in charge, are you? Someone else is. Who?"

Carmen shook her head. "Someone more powerful than you could ever imagine."

"So, why are you here then? To finish the job?" Mark asked.

"Something like that. What did the professor tell you about the *Hawk*?" she asked.

"Not much, we were meant to go back today. Which we did and we know how that turned out."

She nodded. "I suppose it is a waste of time asking you where Miss Reynolds is?"

He shrugged. "Maybe. Tell me something, how does a nice looking broad like you get mixed up with a bunch of cutthroats?"

Carmen smiled. It was a 'You'll never find out' smile. "I can see I'm wasting my time here. We will make an example of you for your people. Maybe if they see what happens to those who interfere, they will stop this silly quest. The police will take you soon to a quiet place where you will be taken care of."

Mark sighed. "Maybe in another life we could have been friends."

She shook her head. "I doubt it. Have a nice death."

"You, too."

————

Brooke and Anika sat across the street from the police station and watched the woman leave. "That's her," Brooke said.

"Who?" Anika asked.

"She tried to kill us in our room. Do you know her?"

"Her name is Carmen. She runs a security team for

the Order. Apparently, she is very good at what she does."

"She is," Brooke told her. "She kicked our asses."

Anika took out her Glock and checked its loads. She reached for the door handle and Brooke grabbed her arm. "Wait."

There was movement at the entrance to the police station and three officers emerged escorting Mark. "It looks like they are taking him out to dispose of him," Anika said.

"That makes it easier for us to get him," Brooke pointed out.

Anika's face grew serious. "Yes, it does."

They waited as Mark was loaded into a car and began to follow as the vehicle pulled out onto the street. Anika left several cars between them so she was not too close. The police vehicle drove through the city to the outskirts where they reached a landfill site.

Brooke said, "I've seen this once before."

"Where?"

"Television show, can't remember what it was."

"Maybe they have, too."

"Maybe. Let's go get Mark."

———

In handcuffs, Mark was dragged from the back of the police vehicle. The men marched him across to where a bulldozer sat idle and stood him in front of its large shiny blade. Walking away about ten feet, they turned to face him.

Mark called out to them, "What! No last cigarette? No meal? I must say, you guys aren't very good hosts. Your hospitality leaves a lot to be desired."

They stared at him and drew their weapons.

"I hope you are good shots."

Still, they said nothing. When they'd taken him from the cell, he'd noticed their tattoos. Like Carmen, these guys were part of the Order.

"I must say one thing though," Mark continued. "You're mighty careless about what you do."

They raised their weapons.

Mark closed his eyes.

Then came the gunfire.

Mark cracked an eye open and saw the dead policemen lying on the ground in the dirt. He then looked up at Brooke and Anika. "Never thought I'd see the day."

"Don't get too excited," Brooke said. "It's a one-off."

He looked at Anika. "It's been a minute."

"You look well. But now I must go. Be careful, the Spanish Order are not done with you yet."

Anika walked away and Mark looked questioningly at Brooke. "What the hell was that?"

She shook her head. "I have no idea."

———

Berlin, Germany

They were all gathered around the large desk in the briefing room. Webster was still in his chair, Krause, his arm in plaster, and Johann had his in a sling to protect his collarbone.

Schmidt ran his gaze over his people and said, "Right, we've had a few days. Now what have we come up with?"

Grace said, "Mr. Webster and I have been researching the Spanish Order. Like we were told, they date back to the sixteenth century. However, we found threads of their existence right up until now."

"We learned that the hard way," Mark said.

"The Order, along with their piracy, has survived the ages," Grace continued. "They boarded merchant ships and stole cargo; private vessels, treasure hunters and their boats vanished, all are said to have been raided by mysterious pirates. Whoever it was left no witnesses."

Molly said, "I've been through the professor's diary, and he has documented events like this as well. The difference, however, is that he found a survivor—a witness. A young Italian woman who was on a yacht with her friends in the Med. A boat with armed men came out of the night fog and boarded them, killing everyone on board. All except the girl. She went over the side and hung off a rope while they ransacked the yacht. One of them came to the side and leaned on the rail. In the light from the yacht, she saw a tattoo on his arm. Once they were done, they threw everyone over the side and scuttled the yacht."

"How did she survive?" Mark asked.

"She found a Styrofoam cooler which stayed afloat on the surface. She was picked up the following day by a passing boat."

"What happened when she told them what happened?"

"The authorities figured she was lying, and that being young, everyone in the group were drunk, and the boat sank. There was a search, but nothing was ever found."

"And now they are high tech," Brooke said. "Werner, did you find anything on the *Hawk* in the Med?"

"Nothing documented."

"It was a longshot, I guess. What about the diary?"

"In the professor's investigations he came across that documentation of the sighting. He also mentioned a port where two ships anchored for a while but there was sickness on board."

"What port?" Mark asked.

"Algiers."

"Makes sense. Algiers was a haven for pirates around that time."

"Then you go to Algiers," Schmidt said. "I have an old friend there who may be able to help. He's British actually. We'll stay in Berlin and see what else we can come up with."

Brooke nodded. "We can do that. But this time we go prepared."

"I'm all for prepared," agreed Mark.

————

Algiers

Algiers sat on the edge of the Mediterranean where it had started life as a small port in Carthage. After the Punic wars it was taken over by the Romans and named Icosium. Over time it changed hands most violently. Then by the time 1541 came around it was a hot bed of Barbary Pirates where piracy and ransom were the order of the day.

"At least our plane didn't crash," Mark said as he dumped his bag beside the sofa in the hotel suite.

"I'll put that down as a plus," Brooke replied as she walked over to the French doors onto the balcony. She opened them and went outside, looking over the rail and down onto the street.

"Looking for old friends?" Mark asked as he took his P30 from pants and sat it on the table.

Brooke came back inside and nodded. "Always. I'm

still trying to work out why Anika helped us and who this elusive Carmen is."

"Since our meeting with Johann's friend isn't until tomorrow, shall we take in some of the city?" Mark asked.

Brooke stared at him. "Why do I feel that I'm going to regret saying yes?"

"With an attitude like that you will," Mark said and picked up his P30.

Leaving the room, they traveled down in the elevator, and out through the lobby. Brooke scanned it as they walked through, checking to see if there was anything she should be worried about.

Once they hit the street, Mark asked, "Which way?"

Brooke grinned at him. "The safest way."

"You, my dear, are funny."

"Yes, but I'm still alive."

———

"They are in Algiers, Carmen." The voice was harsher than usual.

She closed her eyes. *Go away.* "I know where they are, Father, I can see them."

"Then do something about it," he hissed. "No, on second thoughts, stay out of the way. I will have my people take care of them."

Anger flared inside the woman. "Your people? You have your people here?"

"When things aren't handled in the correct manner, sometimes one must take care of situations himself."

"I told you I would take care of it, Father."

"And yet you haven't," he replied bitterly. "So, now, just stay out of the way, Carmen. My people will handle

it. I do not want these Foundation people ruining everything now."

"You are making a mistake."

"It is mine to make."

When the call disconnected, Carmen said into her
comms, "Everyone, stand down."

"What is happening?" Marco asked from the driver's
seat of the Mercedes.

"My father has ordered us to stop what we're doing,"
she said fiercely. "His people will take care of it."

Her bodyguard nodded. "What do we do now?"

Her emerald eyes flared with anger. "Take me back to
the hotel and fuck me. I've had enough of today."

———

Soon after departing the hotel, Brooke and Mark came
across an alley filled with market stalls which they
checked while passing through. There were towering
baskets of fresh produce along with many vendors selling
aromatic servings of hot food. Further along there were
many stalls showing crafts of mats and clothing, all hand
made.

Mark was about to try some local cuisine when
Brooke said, "I wouldn't advise it."

"Why?"

"You'll be up all night trying to soothe the ring of fire
it'll give you."

Mark knew what she was talking about. "Good
point."

They kept walking and made it out the other end of
the alley. As they turned right, they noticed a long line
of busy cafes and restaurants along each side of the
street. Brooke kept checking surreptitiously to see if they
were being followed and was unable to locate anyone,

but her gut told her differently. Shortly after, she spotted them.

"I damn well knew it," she said in a low voice. "We just should have stayed in our room."

"How many?" Mark asked.

"I have two following us on the opposite side of the street," she replied.

"Yes, I've got two behind us."

"Can you see her?" Brooke asked.

"The redhead? No. These could be different people. What about from Stuber?"

"It's possible, I guess."

Mark had another look. "No, these guys look totally different. Beards, long hair."

Brooke scanned their surroundings. Each sidewalk was loaded with pedestrians, the four followers blending with the masses for cover. Up ahead on the left she saw a café. "Must be coffee time."

"You want coffee now?" Mark asked, not catching on.

Brooke shrugged. "I think better when I drink coffee."

"Fine, let's drink coffee."

They moved quickly without rushing into the coffee shop, sitting at a table towards the back where they could see out the front window. Moments later, a waitress approached them to take their order. While this happened, two of their pursuers remained across the street while the others moved towards a table behind them. The pair ordered coffee too. One of them had an English accent, while the other sounded Italian.

"What do you think we should do when we find the ship?" Brooke asked loud enough for the two men seated behind them to overhear.

"We'll have to report it to the Worldwide Treasure Hunter's Committee," Mark replied.

Brooke glared at him.

"Or not," he added.

The scent of fresh coffee and cakes wafted through the café. Their coffees came and they sat drinking and talking about nothing in particular. They were almost finished when a woman sat down at their table. Mark stared at her and shook his head. "You're just everywhere, aren't you?"

Anika Meyer smiled at them. "You can thank me later."

6

SHIPS IN THE NIGHT

Algiers

Anika had picked them up in the market. First the original pair, and then the next two. She kept her distance and only decided to show herself when Brooke and Mark sat to have coffee.

"Is this what you plan on doing?" Brooke asked her in a low voice. "Follow us everywhere we go?"

"You might think that this is a good idea once this is over," Anika said. She reached out and brushed a hand against Mark's cheek affectionately. "Besides, I'm starting to become attached to our mutual friend here. It would be a shame to lose him."

Mark smiled mirthlessly at her. "You know, in another life I might just ask you out, take you home, and then screw the ass off you."

"In another life, I might just let you," Anika replied, batting her lashes at him.

"If you two are done fantasizing," Brooke said, "we have another issue at hand."

"I can fix that," Anika said and got to her feet.

"What are you doing?" Brooke asked, but the German woman ignored her.

Instead, she turned and sat at the table with the two men who'd been tailing Brooke and Mark.

"Hello, gentlemen, how is your day going?"

"What do you want?" the one with the English accent asked.

Anika nodded. "Good, straight to the point. I like that. Under the table, when I sat down, I drew my Glock. Right at this moment it is pointed at your friend's balls. Now, what is going to happen is you both are going to get up and leave. And you will take your friends across the street with you."

"Bitch! Are you crazy?" the Englishman hissed.

"No. Just to show you that I am not, I will point out the disadvantage you are at." Anika nodded across the street. "The man there with the newspaper is one of mine. Two more in the café along the street. The woman who is walking along the opposite side of the street with the headphones on, also mine. So, make your choice. You can die here or live to fight another day."

The Italian glared at her. "You have made a very big mistake."

Anika's smile grew colder. "Tell your boss that Kurt Stuber says hello."

The pair of unhappy operatives stood up and walked away. Across the street the other two followed suit.

Anika came back to the table where Brooke and Mark sat. Mark said, "That'll work."

"Not for long, they'll regroup and then come back after you."

"We'll be ready," Brooke stated, more than a little peeved that she had allowed them to end up in such a situation in the first place. "What are you doing here, Anika?"

"Waiting for you to find the treasure so we can steal it."

Brooke looked at Mark who just shrugged.

"There is one other thing as well," Anika said.

"What's that?"

"A month ago, some people boarded a ship named the *Venetian Sea*. They took something from it before it was sunk in the middle of the Med. Officially there was an explosion in the engine room, and it went to the bottom with all hands. Unofficially, it was scuttled."

Brooke stared at her. "What was taken?"

"The ship was on route to Indonesia to be scrapped," Anika explained. "At the last moment while it was docked in Spain it was given a last-minute cargo destined for India. They were sailing for Suez when they were attacked, and their cargo stolen."

"What was the cargo?" Mark repeated Brooke's question.

"Nuclear material," Brooke said before Anika could reply. "My guess is spent fuel rods. Something they could make a huge ass dirty bomb with. Or several."

"Be stuffed," Mark hissed. "They took nuclear material?"

Anika nodded. "Yes, before they sank the ship."

"Who?"

"The Spanish Order," Brooke said. "It was them, wasn't it?"

Anika's expression was uncertain. "Maybe. Kurt isn't sure."

"Why are you telling us this?"

"Because I would hate to see you suffer the affects of radioactive poisoning if you should accidentally come into contact with it."

"You mean, who would find the treasure for you if we weren't around?" Brooke said.

"Yes." She got up from the table. "Now I must go. Good luck. And be careful. I cannot be around all the time to help you."

Anika walked away and disappeared into the foot traffic. "Close your mouth, Mark, you're drooling."

"I think I'm in love," he replied.

"You do remember who she is, right?"

He nodded. "Oh yes."

"Idiot."

———

The hotter Carmen became, the more her freckles stood out against her skin. And, at that point in time, her freckles seemed to glow. Much like the rest of her from the anger which smoldered just below the surface. Even sex hadn't dampened the fire.

"I'm sorry, Marco," she apologized. "I didn't mean to be so rough."

Marco licked the blood from his lip where she'd bitten down on it, its coppery taste sitting on his tongue. "It is fine, Carmen."

She sighed. "No, no it isn't. I shouldn't take my frustrations out on you."

"Who would you take them out on if not for me?" he asked her.

"I do not know."

He nodded at the red dressing on her shoulder. "I think you might need that looked at."

Carmen looked at her shoulder. "After I shower," she replied. "Come and join me."

"I'm not sure I could take another one of your—"

"I promise I will be gentle."

"Then how can I refuse?"

An hour later Carmen's cell rang. "Yes?"

She listened patiently and then disconnected. She turned to look at Marco. "They failed. My father's magnificent fucking men failed."

Marco stared at her in silence.

"But get this," she continued, "there is a new player on the block."

Marco frowned. "Who?"

"Kurt Stuber."

———

"I don't like it," Schmidt said. "Villains are coming out of the woodwork, and we can't even see them until they're on top of us."

"I'm sorry, Johann, I'll—"

He cut Brooke off. "No, I do not blame you. I think, though, it would be better if we gave it a miss."

"No. We must keep going."

"Brooke—"

"We have to be on the right path, Johann," she said to him. "We keep going."

"What about the nuclear material?" Schmidt asked.

"We don't even know if it is true. All we have is the word of a woman who would kill us when our backs are turned. I don't even think it has been reported."

"Just be careful, Brooke."

"We will, sir."

She cut the call and heard the shower water stop running. Minutes later Mark emerged with only a towel wrapped around him. "Shower is free."

"I think I might just indulge," she replied.

Brooke took her top off, revealing a black bra and a line of Latin writing on her ribs. *Donec pugnare non potes pugnare amplius.*

"What does that mean?" Mark asked.

"It's Latin," Brooke said.

"Yes, but what does it mean?"

"Basically, it translates as fight until you can't fight anymore."

He nodded. "I like it."

Brooke took her jeans off and Mark caught a glimpse of just how athletic she was. Yes, sir, he liked the view but—

"Are you staring at me, Mark?" she asked, turning to look at him.

"No, not really."

"Comparing me to your German admirer, maybe?"

"I'll admit, you're easy on the eye but you're not my type," he said.

"Really, what is your type?" Brooke asked.

"Someone who's not my boss."

Brooke gave him a grin laced with satisfaction. "Good answer."

"You want some room service?" Mark asked.

"Sure."

"Any preferences?" Mark asked.

"You choose. We'll see how much notice you take. Just make sure it isn't pasta."

Brooke went to the shower and turned on the faucets. She took her underwear off and climbed in. The water was hot and felt like small needles piercing her skin. Instead of adding more cold water, she turned it hotter.

Brooke picked up the soap and used it all over her body except for her hair. She just used the water for that. Once she was done, she turned the water off, allowing the excess to sluice off, then climbed out.

Grabbing a fluffy white town from the rail, she ran it over her dripping hair first, rubbing it over her face and arms before wrapping it around herself. Then she went out into the main room they were sharing.

And found herself staring at several visitors.

"Shit."

———

"Wow, this is awkward," Brooke said. "If I'd known we were going to have visitors I would have dressed."

"Sorry," said Mark. "I forgot to mention they were coming."

They were the two men who'd been seated behind them at the café that afternoon. Now they were here in their room with guns in their hands. "Put your hands up," the Englishman said.

Brooke gave him an exasperated look. "You do realize that if I let go of this towel it will drop to the floor and— well you can guess the rest."

"I think you should do as they say," Mark said to her with a smirk.

She glared at him. "You would."

"If I'm going to die, I'd rather the last thing that I see be you rather than these pricks."

"You're just like all the rest, aren't you?" Her voice went up. "Fucking objectifying women. I bet you watch porn all the time too."

"What's wrong with that?" Mark asked. "I'm a healthy red-blooded American male."

"Pervert more like it."

Now Mark's voice elevated. "I take offence at that."

"I take fucking offence at you," Brooke shot back at him.

Now they were arguing.

"Hey!" the Englishman shouted. "Get your fucking hands up."

And Brooke did.

And the towel fell.

And Mark moved.

While the two men were distracted by Brooke, Mark launched himself at the Italian who was the closest. Mark raised his forearm using his elbow as a weapon. He brought it around just before impact so that all his force came down from the shoulder and exploded into the man's jaw.

Mark heard the jaw break with an audible crunch. The Italian dropped like a stone, releasing his grip on the weapon. It thumped to the floor beside its owner. Mark dived for it and scooped it up. The Englishman turned to fire when Brooke picked up a solid glass fruit bowl from the coffee table and threw it.

The heavy object crashed into the side of his head. The Englishman fell like a tree in the forest, the bowl shattering on the floor. Mark removed the man's weapon from reach and checked for a pulse. Like his friend, he was out to it.

"Both are unconscious."

"Good. Get someone up here who can deal with them while I get some clothes on. You might want to get dressed yourself, muscles."

"Yes, you could be right."

————

"Fucking asshole," Carmen almost screamed as she threw her cell at the wall.

"What is it?" Marco asked.

"He tried again—his people tried again, and they screwed it up, *again*. This is getting beyond a damn joke."

"What do we do?"

"Fix up his mistakes."

————

Professor Solomon Bush's specialty was Algeria in the Middle Ages. He was a man in his early fifties who'd lived and worked in Algiers for the past twenty-five years. He'd met Johann Schmidt at a conference in Berlin some twenty years earlier and the two had hit it off immediately. Brooke and Mark met him at the Algiers Museum of Antiquities.

"Professor Bush?"

The professor smiled. "That's me, my dear. Solomon Bush at your service. You must be Brooke Reynolds and Mark Butler"

"Yes, sir."

His eyes focused on Mark. "I knew your father, son, I'm sorry to hear what happened to him."

"Thank you."

"Johann told me you were here about something to do with the *Golden Hawk*. Is that right?"

Brooke nodded. "Yes, that's right. We're following a lead."

"Come with me."

He took them to the cafeteria where they sat down with coffees. Strong, black, bitter. "All right, tell me what you have."

Brooke took him through everything from the beginning. The cross, the plane crash, the Spanish Order, the diary, and the death of Emelio Carris.

"Oh crap," Bush growled. "I knew Emilio. Nice chap. Very good at what he did. So he was sure that the *Hawk* came here?"

"It wasn't named as such, but two ships arrived at a port near here with sickness aboard them."

"What date?"

"Early sixteen seventy-two," Mark said.

Bush finished his coffee and placed the cup on the table. "Let's see if we can find something."

They followed as he set off through the museum and down a staircase into a large basement. He walked them to a solid steel door with armed guards standing either side. Mark said, "I'm starting to get The Librarian vibes."

Bush put in a code and the doors opened.

And revealed a vault which seemed to go on forever.

"Yes, sir, straight out of the movie," Mark said in wonderment.

"There are over a thousand years of history in here," Bush said. "Now, let's see if we can find your ship."

An hour later, they had what they needed. "I have something here which may be of interest," Bush said, holding up a yellowed piece of vellum in a gloved hand. "According to this, the ships did come. With them came disease, and the people drove the crews away. Forced them back out to sea."

"Does it have any indication of where they went?" Brooke asked.

"No. This explains that it was nighttime."

Mark said, "At least we're on the right track."

"What we need is another thread to pull," Brooke said. "We give this information to the rest of the team and see what they can come up with."

"What do we do in the meantime?" Mark asked.

"Find a new place to stay." Brooke turned to Bush. "Thank you for all you've done, Professor."

"It wasn't much. If I can think of anything else, I'll let you know."

"Thank you."

They made their way back through the museum, glancing around every time a display caught their eye. When they walked out onto the street, they climbed into their silver Audi A8, with Mark behind the wheel.

Brooke said, "I don't know why we had to have this expensive thing."

"Might as well go in comfort."

"Just drive."

He pulled away from the curb and into sparse traffic. As the automatic gear box went up a gear, Mark noticed the black BMW pull out and begin to follow them. "Why can't these guys just give up?"

"What is it?"

"We've got a tail."

Brooke checked the mirror on her side and saw the vehicle. "Yeah, two of them, I think."

"I bet they're our old friends."

From an alley just ahead of their position, a van rocketed towards them and skidded to a stop, blocking their path. The side door slid open and two shooters with automatic weapons emerged from the opening.

Mark trod on the brakes and the Audi came to a shuddering halt. "Shit, this is bad."

Brooke took out her P30 as Mark threw the Audi in reverse for all of two wheel cycles before he braked once again. "Yeah, no, we're not going that way."

The men in the van opened fire and bullets sprayed the Audi.

Mark floored the accelerator as the windscreen disintegrated. They both ducked below the level of the dash, Mark using the display from the reversing camera to guide him.

Brooke stuck her gun-filled hand up and fired back, her bullets flying wildly.

"That's not going to help," Mark shouted.

"It makes me fucking feel better," she snarled in response.

The rear end of the Audi hit the front quarter panel of the BMW. As it did, Mark floored the gas pedal to give the vehicle a better chance of pushing the heavier one out of the way.

Brooke twisted in the seat and fired at the second vehicle. While Mark worked the wheel, he said, "Boy is Johann going to be pissed."

More bullets punched into the Audi. "You need to get your shit together, genius, and get us the hell out of here."

Mark selected drive and floored the gas pedal once more. The wheel spun and the rear end snapped around, the pock marked nose now pointed back the other way. Mark saw a narrow gap between the wall and the BMW and drove the Audi at it. It wasn't wide enough to get through, but he wedged the car into the opening and the vehicle's momentum did the rest.

It forced the vehicle aside and kept on going. Moments later they turned a corner and they were alone. Brooke looked over at Mark. "Are you all right?"

"Yeah, that was damn intense, though."

Returning the damaged vehicle to a stunned customer service agent at the hire company, Mark smiled at the woman behind the counter and said, "I think the insurance should cover it."

7

KISSING THE ENEMY

Algiers

"What do you have?" Schmidt asked that evening over the video call streamed into the conference room in Berlin.

Brooke said, "The ships were here but they were forced to move on. They brought disease with them, and the locals weren't happy about it. We figure that if someone can crosscheck the timeline with disease outbreaks, we might get something."

"I'll see what I can come up with," said Werner.

"Johann, there is something else you should know. Anika Meyer is still around." She went on to tell him about what had transpired over the preceding days. "We're grateful for the help, but the ulterior motive stands out like the proverbial…"

"Yes, just be careful. The Order are a dangerous lot. We're trying to narrow it down, but they're like ghosts."

"Is there any news about the *Venetian Sea*?" Mark asked.

Grace Cramer's face appeared. "I did some digging

through my contacts and, although it's still all very hush hush, it would seem that the veracity can be confirmed."

"Great."

"Oh, there was something else. The pictures you sent through, it would seem that every person is dead."

"Come again?"

"They're dead, the certificates say so."

"Shit."

Johann said, "Hang in there. I'll send you through whatever we can come up with. Give it a couple of days. If nothing more is found, come back to Berlin and we'll work another angle. Talk later."

The call terminated, and Mark flopped back on the sofa with his arm over his head as though in a swoon. After several moments, he sat up suddenly and said, "I'm going out for something to eat. You want anything?"

"I'll be fine. I'm going to turn in soon. Don't be late and do be careful."

"I'll be fine," Mark said stuffing his P30 into his pants.

"Watch that don't go off, slick."

Mark chuckled and left the hotel room.

Hoping that this hotel was safer than the last, he jounced down the stairs, walking along the street before finding a restaurant that looked interesting. He was taken to a table where he ordered a lamb dish called Al-Shetitha. Unsure about it at first, it took several mouthfuls before he got to a point where he was enjoying it.

When he was halfway through his meal, he paused to look up as Anika Meyer slipped into the seat opposite him. Mark shook his head. "How did I know you were going to appear?"

She smiled at him. "I hate seeing anyone eat alone. Besides, maybe you secretly wanted me to show."

"Are you alone?" Mark asked, raising an eyebrow.

"Maybe."

He turned his head both ways, glancing around the restaurant. "Maybe you are."

She signaled the waiter over. "I'll have what he's having."

The waiter nodded and walked away.

"So, what is it that you want, Anika?" Mark asked.

"How goes the investigation?" she asked with a smile.

"Slowly."

"Anything I can do to help?"

"Tell me who is behind the Order?"

"Oh, sweetie, If I do that, we would lose all our fun."

He noticed the spark of amusement as he looked into her eyes. "This isn't a game, Anika. These people stole nuclear material."

"You are being way too dramatic," she replied, waving a hand to brush off his concern.

Mark opened his mouth to speak, paused, and then he had an epiphany. "You have no idea who they are, do you?"

She reached across the table, dipped her finger into the sauce on his plate and sucked it off. Then she said, "Apart from Carmen, no damn idea. And it was only luck that we came across her and her security team."

"Shit. Could she have raided the *Venetian Sea*?"

"It's possible."

They let the silence hang over them as they each contemplated that.

"Maybe we can help each other. Tell me what you know."

Mark chuckled. "You know more about them than we do. All we know is that dead people are trying to kill us."

"Why?"

"It has to be something to do with the treasure," Mark said, forking some food into his mouth.

"I think we should go," Anika said, her tone a little tense.

"I'm not finished, and your meal hasn't arrived yet."

"Yes, you are," she replied. "Are you armed?"

The question made him stop and stare at her, answering any questions he had. "Yes."

"It would seem I have been careless. Two men have just entered the restaurant. They have been following my team on and off. It appears that they mean business this time."

Mark glanced over his shoulder and saw them. "I see. Kitchen?"

Anika nodded. "Maybe that would be best."

As he got to his feet, Mark said, "You owe me a dinner."

They moved swiftly towards the swinging door which led into the restaurant's kitchen. Mark pushed through and found a myriad of cooks and kitchen staff busily working over hot plates and grills. Mark spotted a door on the far side of the kitchen and started towards it.

A chef brandishing a knife stepped in front of him. He spoke rapidly and Mark had no hope of understanding him. Instead, he hit the man in the stomach and relieved him of the knife, placing it on the work bench. As Mark moved past the gagging man, he patted him on the shoulder. "Sorry, buddy."

Anika followed him through the doorway just as their two pursuers appeared. She nudged Mark and said, "Go faster."

They quickened their pace and soon found themselves sprinting down a long hallway towards a closed door at the end of it.

Mark crashed against it, turning the handle at the same time. The door sprang open under the impact, and they emerged into a dark alley filled with stinking garbage.

"This way," Anika said, pointing to their right.

The pair began running. Mark heard the same door crash back and a shout chased them along the alley.

Gunfire sounded from behind them as the two pursuers discharged weapons. The crack of bullets echoed in the alley as they passed close by.

"I'm sick of this shit," Mark said and took out his P30.

He turned and dropped into a crouch. Taking aim he opened fire, watching as one of the shooters fell to the ground with a thud. The second man threw out his arms as a round impacted his chest, and he landed in a tangle of arms and legs.

"Good shooting," Anika said.

Bright headlights slashed through the darkness of the alley ahead of them, almost blinding them as they ran. The vehicle's revving engine echoed along the alley, and they knew immediately that they were in trouble.

Anika brought out her own firearm. A Glock P9. She stood her ground and opened fire. In the high beams she looked like an angel of death unleashing at least half a magazine before the van turned violently to the left and slammed into the wall of a building.

Although Mark had never seen it happen apart from in the movies—he felt as though he was watching a rerun of the A-Team—the van lurched into the air and twisted as it continued forward. It crashed down, the sound of grinding metal and shattering glass reaching his ears.

"That'll ruin your day, sure as shit," he said to Anika.

"Come on, let's go."

They ran back the other way and were soon out on the street, putting their guns away to not draw attention. The traffic was flowing both ways and it appeared as though there were no more would-be killers to worry about.

Mark looked at Anika and said, "I'd best be going back to the hotel."

She fixed him with her stare and asked, "Why?"

———

The first time was over in no time at all. Just a wrestle of arms and legs and everything else animalistic as their passion poured out like lava from a hollow crater. Then they rested for a while before going at it again, taking their time and enjoying the sensual nature of their coupling. After their synchronous climaxes, Mark lay beside Anika whose head was resting on his chest. "That was unexpected," he said to her.

She lifted her head to look at him, the dark eyeliner around her eyes standing out. "You know it wasn't. You wanted it as much as I did."

"OK, I admit it. What will your boss say?"

"He will try to use it to his advantage," she said languidly.

"What will you do?" His tone was asking if she would do it.

"I may be a lot of things, Mark, but I would not use sex to turn you. Besides, it will never happen again."

He looked at the ceiling of the hotel room and felt the chill of the air conditioning teasing his skin. "Where is the Amber Room?"

She hit him in the ribs, solidly.

"Oof! What was that?"

"You did not just ask me that," Anika growled. "Not after I said I would not use sex against you. Especially if you want this to happen again."

"You just said—"

"Shut up, I know what I said."

"You know this will end badly," Mark pointed out. "Especially if we're on opposite sides of a gun fight."

"I would expect you to shoot me, Mark, just as I would you."

"OK, this suddenly feels fucked up."

"Why? We are two people using each other to get what we want."

"Then tell me about the Amber Room."

Anika was quiet for a moment before saying, "All right, it is being slowly assembled. Like a jigsaw. The Nazis were most careful with it, and it is in pristine condition. And that is all I'm saying. Now, how did you survive that plane crash?"

"We were damn lucky."

"Yes."

Mark sat up and swung his legs over the side of the bed. Anika frowned. "Where are you going?"

"Back to my hotel. Brooke will be wondering where I am."

"Do you like her?"

He stood and turned. "Are you jealous?"

"No. Get dressed and get out."

Mark grinned and climbed back on the bed and started to kiss her. He pulled back and smiled at her. Anika became angrier with him. "Get out."

———

"Where were you?" Brooke asked the following morning.

"I went out for dinner, I told you."

She stared at Mark. "You were with her."

"Her, who?"

"You know who I'm talking about, Mark. Fucking Anika. You slept with her?"

"It wasn't planned, it just happened. After the shootout and all. Adrenaline rush, you know how it is."

"Back up a bit. What shootout?"

He filled her in on the events of the previous evening. "It was a close-run thing."

Brooke was still angry but deep down she was relieved that he was all right. "How can I trust you, Mark, when you're sleeping with the enemy?"

"I seem to remember a movie—"

"Grow the fuck up," she snarled.

"I did find out some information," Mark told her.

"What?"

"They are rebuilding the Amber Room."

"Where?" Brooke was taken aback at the unexpected answer and couldn't hide the excitement in her voice.

"I don't know, but she said it was in pristine condition."

"You could have gotten something worthwhile."

Mark said, "What I got was all right."

Brooke glared at him. Mark raised his eyebrows. "Too soon?"

"Way too soon. Shit, what the hell am I going to tell Johann?"

"Nothing, because you can still trust me, Brooke. I promise."

———

Due to his arm in the sling, Werner supervised while Molly did all the work. It was faster than him trying to type one handed. The screen on her computer changed and said: *No Results Found!*

"This is like looking for a needle in a bloody haystack," she growled sounding exasperated. "There is nothing at all in archives, historical records, yadda, yadda, yadda."

Werner frowned. He wasn't about to let it beat him. There had to be something somewhere.

"How goes it?" Grace Cramer asked as she approached them.

"If we were making any more progress we'd be going backwards," Molly replied.

Werner turned and looked at her. "There has to be something somewhere. How are your inquiries going?"

"Much the same as yours. The Spanish Order are ghosts, literally."

A light suddenly came on in Werner's head. "The church."

"What?"

Grace asked.

"The church was big on keeping records back in the day. They were like the first rule of law in the early times and kept lots of records. They still do."

Molly tapped at her keys. "You're right. All we have to do is key in the right search parameters and we'll eventually find what we need."

For the next few minutes Molly weaved her magic before printing off an A4 sheet of paper and passing it to Werner. "There is our answer."

"Blast, you're good at what you do."

"What is it?" Grace asked.

Werner handed across the paper. "During the time frame we're looking at there was an outbreak of disease on Sicily. Not that we can be certain, but it is a possibility. It's a lead that can't be ignored."

"So, you're saying that it's a good possibility the ship was there?" Grace ventured.

Werner nodded. "I say it's more than a possibility."

Molly took out her cell and dialed.

"Hi," Brooke answered on the other end.

Molly spoke succinctly, "Go to Sicily. I'll send you what we know."

————

Brooke looked at Mark. "We're going to Sicily. Molly has found something there to do with the church."

"Fair enough," Mark replied. "Hopefully we'll be able to shake loose of our hostile friends."

"Don't count on it."

Mark nodded. "Yeah, you're right. Too much to ask."

————

When Carmen's cell rang, she knew immediately who it was. "Yes, father?"

"I have a job for you, Carmen," her father spoke smoothly. "You and your people."

"If you can't remember, I'm currently in the middle of something. That thing that *your* people failed to take care of."

"It will wait," he told her. "And don't take that tone with me, Princess."

Carmen sighed resignedly as she watched the hotel where Mark and Brooke were staying. "What is it?"

"I need a new scientist," her father told her.

"What happened to the last one?"

"He died. Too much radiation exposure."

"That will happen when you don't put measures in place."

"I don't need your approval, daughter," he snapped. "Just get me my scientist. He is in Rome. I will send you the address."

"Yes, father."

"Thank you."

The call disconnected and Carmen turned and looked at Cosimo. "We need to go to Rome."

"What are we to do there?"

"It seems my father's carelessness has led to the death of his scientist. Now he wants us to bring him a replacement."

Cosimo stared at Carmen. "What does he have planned, anyway?"

She shook her head. "I have no idea. But whatever it is, it will not be good."

8

ESCALATION

Bay of Heights, Sicily

Mark threw his bag on the single bed of the flop house and said, "Well, this is shit."

Brooke tossed hers onto the one beside it. "It's called laying low."

Mark looked at the bed and figured it was about six inches off the floor. "Yeah, I'd definitely call it that."

Along with the bunks the space held a small table, a shower with green mold growing on the grout lines and a faucet that leaked constantly. Mark continued. "I bet we'll need to use body heat to keep warm."

"If it comes to that, sunshine, you'll die of hypothermia."

"Aww, now I know we have to lay low but how low does that need to be, especially when someone from here steals the SUV out the front?"

"No one will do that," she said. "The Capozzis will see to that."

"Who are the Capozzis?" Mark asked.

"Local Mafia."

Mark rechecked his P30. "Just great. Not only do we have pirates to contend with, but the local horse head people as well."

"You worry too much."

They had arrived in Sicily six hours earlier, hiring a vehicle for the drive out of Catania and along the coast. Their destination was a small town where they would find the Church of Jesuits. Johann had chartered a plane to get them to Sicily. The hope was that the church would provide them with the information they needed to reveal what happened to the *Golden Hawk*.

Molly had informed them their contact person was Father Ignatius. He was the longest-serving priest there and was also the unofficial historian for the region.

Mark put the P30 under his pillow. "What are we eating tonight, oh great one?"

"When in Rome…," Brooke replied.

"We're not in Rome, though," Mark pointed out.

"Maybe so, but I'm sure we'll be able to find a decent pizza."

She was right. They went out and found a small café complete with small round tables and red and white checkered tablecloths. Just like the movies. And they served pizza the way it was meant to be served. Home-made with all fresh ingredients supplied by locals. "No pineapple on these babies," Mark said as he picked up another slice.

"I'm quite sure if you asked for something like that here, they would shoot you," Brooke retorted.

"Or wake up with a horse's head in my bed. Bella would be right at home here," Mark theorized.

"More than you would think," Brooke replied.

Mark frowned. "What do you mean?"

"Have you ever seen her tattoo?" Brooke asked.

Mark was suddenly very curious. "What tattoo?"

Brooke shook her head. "Forget that. To see it, she would have to have her clothes off."

"What tattoo?" Mark's interest was piqued.

"She has one of a small dove."

"So?"

"It is a mafia mark," Brooke explained.

"Our little angel is tied to the mafia?" Mark asked incredulously.

"Uh, huh," Brooke said with a nod as she took a bite of her pizza. She pulled it clear of her mouth and strands of mozzarella stretched until they broke.

"Who would have thought?" Mark said almost in awe.

"It's not discussed, as you can tell. She's actually embarrassed about it, so don't let on I told you."

"My lips are sealed," Mark replied with a grin.

"Mark."

"I promise."

"Good."

"And my door will be locked."

Brooke glared at him. "Mark."

He grinned. "Hey, I'd hate to wake up with a horse head in my bed."

"Can't be much different to Anika Meyer," Brooke replied.

"Point taken but that was different."

"Whatever."

Once the pizza was gone, they washed it down with beer before heading back to the place they were staying.

"At least our wheels are still here," Mark said with disbelief.

As they approached the room door, Brooke noticed that it was slightly ajar. She took out her P30 and Mark followed her lead. Using hand signals, she indicated that she would go in first while he covered her rear. With a nod, Mark waited for her to make a move.

Brooke kicked the door back and entered, her weapon raised. "Ah, shit!" she exclaimed and lowered the P30.

"Hi," said Isabella. "Johann thought you might want some help. I'm glad I got the right room. By the way, your lock is busted."

———

"What have we missed?" Brooke asked.

Isabella sipped her beer. "My headaches are mostly gone. Webster is still a pain in the ass, but Grace keeps him in line. The others are mending. Speaking of Grace, she's really cool. You did well selecting her."

"Any news on the pirate front?" Mark asked.

She stared at him. "I don't know, Mark. What about news on the Anika Meyer front?"

He looked at Brooke. "You told her?"

Brooke gave him a guilty look. "Maybe."

"Great. Now I'll wake up with a damn horse head in my bed."

It was Isabella's turn to be surprised. "You told him about my tattoo?"

Exasperation. "I—fine, yes."

"Great."

"How about we get back to business," Brooke growled. "Is there any news on the stolen nuclear waste?"

"Grace reached out to some contacts, and they believe that it is hidden somewhere along the Med coast. Get this, not long after *it* went missing, a nuclear scientist from France disappeared."

"That bodes well," Mark said. "Dirty bomb central coming up."

"Big possibility. What shall we do tomorrow?"

"We're going to the church," Brooke said. "Meet up with Father Ignatius."

"That should be so cool. Old churches have so many artifacts in them. You never know what you'll find. I remember a church in Romania where we once found a chieftain's helmet which dated back to the Getae."

Gone suddenly was the serious young woman, layers peeling back to expose the excited girl who held such a passion for what she did. And she was good at it. Her brain was like a library of information, stored for centuries.

"Where are you sleeping?" Mark asked.

"I'm not sure."

The American sighed. "You can have my bed. I'll share with Brooke."

"Say what?" Brooke said, placing her beer bottle forcefully on the table. "I did not just hear that."

"What? You would want me to sleep on the hard floor?"

She stared at him.

————

"That sucked," Mark said the next morning as he rose from the hard floor. "Brings back memories of my days serving."

Brooke and Isabella were already up and drinking coffee they had got from a café along the street. Brooke put a third steaming paper cup on the table and said, "Try that."

Mark picked it up and took a sip. "I should marry you, you know?"

"Yeah, not going to happen."

After their coffees, they had showers and got ready to head to the church, climbing into the SUV and setting off.

The church building was a large sandstone structure surrounded by pedestals holding marble statuary atop them. Over 1,500 years old, it was decorated with intricate work, and Isabella stood admiring it. "This is magnificent."

The interior was even better, and they stood in awe when they entered, taking in more statues, artworks, dark wood, stained glass, and artifacts collected by the church over centuries.

"Wow," said Isabella. "I have to look."

"Don't get lost," Brooke warned her.

"Oh, please."

A young priest appeared, crossing the narthex to greet Brooke and Mark. "Can I help you?" he asked in Italian.

He spoke pleasantly and looked to have a peaceful demeanor. Brooke nodded. "We're here to see Father Ignatius."

The priest bowed his head slightly and said, "I will just see if he is available."

They waited a few moments before a priest wearing black appeared. Brooke guessed him to be somewhere in his mid-seventies. "Father Ignatius?"

"Yes, my dear."

"I'm Brooke Reynolds, and this is Mark Butler. We're from the Schmidt Foundation."

The old man nodded. "What can I do for you?"

"We were told that you might be able to help us with a ship we're looking for. The *Golden Hawk*?"

He glanced to the side as his mind went deep into thought. "I can't recall the name."

"What about events?" Mark asked. "When it arrived, it brought with it disease."

"When was this?"

"Sixteen seventy-two."

A light seemed to go on inside the old man's head. "Come with me."

He led them down a narrow stone stairway into what appeared to be a large library. Seated at different tables covered in scrolls were three other priests who were scribing. Ignatius said, "The fathers are documenting events over the years. The scrolls they are transcribing from are very fragile, so they are putting all the information into journals. Then the scrolls and parchment will be stored with the utmost care so they are preserved."

Mark stopped and watched one of the priests as he worked carefully. The man must have felt eyes on him because he looked up at Mark and smiled.

Mark said, "Keeping you busy?"

"You have no idea." The priest was English. Seeing Mark's surprise, his smile broadened.

"No shi—no joke."

Mark followed Brooke and Father Ignatius. The priest stopped at a long row of shelves and removed one of the journals. Carrying the large book over to a table, he opened it and began to flick through the pages. "What you are looking for should be in here."

As he scanned the pages the old man started to hum. Something classical by Bach. Then he stopped and began to read the details on a page. "Yes, this is it. It doesn't mention the ships by name, but these are without doubt the ones you are looking for."

"How can you tell?" Mark asked.

"They both had sickness. One was a bigger ship than the other."

"The galleon," Brooke surmised. "The *Golden Hawk*."

"It is possible."

"And they stopped here?"

"No, no. They anchored at Mirabella Bay."

"Where is that?" Brooke asked.

"Another hour along the coast," Father Ignatius said. "There is nothing there except the monastery overlooking the cliffs. The village at the water's edge is no more."

"What happened to the ships and crew?" Mark asked.

The priest went back to reading. "It says that the sick and the rest of the crew were taken to the monastery. The ships were—"

He stopped.

"Yes?" asked Mark, encouraging him to continue.

"The ships were burned."

Mark and Brooke stared at each other. Brooke asked, "Was there any mention of the cargo from the ships?"

Ignatius read some more. He shook his head. "No, nothing."

"There you are," Isabella said seemingly exhausted, yet excited at the same time.

"What is the matter?" Brooke asked.

"Look." She held up a gold chain with an emerald encrusted cross attached to it.

"Oh, no, my dear," Ignatius said aghast. "You cannot touch the artifacts."

"I'm sorry, Father," Isabella said hurriedly in Italian. Then, "This is the Cross of Saint Nathaniel."

"Who?" Mark asked.

"It would take too long to explain, my darling, but just know that the last known place for this item is said to have been on the *Golden Hawk*. It was definitely here."

"Where did the cross come from, Father?" Brooke asked Ignatius.

He shook his head. "I do not know. It has been here for as long as I have."

Brooke nodded. "That's fine. You should put it back, Bella."

"But?"

"Put it back."

Isabella suddenly looked like a scolded child. *Questa è una stronzata assoluta.* An epithet in Italian burst from her clenched jaw, which drew frowns from those around her. She looked at Brooke and said, "This is absolute bull—"

Mark's hand clamped over her mouth before she could finish. "What she means is good day, Father. And thank you."

Ignatius smiled. "When she calms down, tell her she is welcome."

Another muffled outburst spewed forth into Mark's palm as he guided her away towards the stairs which would take them back up into the church. When Mark finally let her go, she whirled around and glared at him. "I should go back and give him a piece of my mind."

"It wouldn't do you any good, Bella," Brooke said. "I know he's lying about the cross, but he's also scared of telling us why."

"So, what do we do?" Bella asked, her hands on hips.

"We go swimming," Brooke replied. "How are your scuba diving skills?"

They emerged from the church onto the street and the practiced eyes of Brooke and Mark picked out their followers right away. Brooke said, "Two at two."

"Another two at our nine," Mark replied.

"Do you think it was the priest?"

"No. Too quick for him."

"Bella, get in the SUV."

She did as ordered without question. Brooke said, "You go left, I'll go right."

"These aren't the same people," Mark told her.

"No, they're dressed all wrong."

Mark followed Brooke's lead and took his P30 from the back of his pants. "I hope God forgives us for taking our guns into the church."

"If you don't duck you might find out."

Mark's eyes narrowed as he saw the newcomers raise weapons and aim in their direction.

"Go!" Brooke barked and they ran in opposite directions.

The men opened fire at the fleeing figures. Mark dived behind a parked vehicle and bullets hammered into it, an erratic and loud form of Morse code. Mark rose and began shooting with the P30. His shots found their target as the windows of the shooter's vehicle exploded. He muttered a curse at his crap shooting and ducked down as the men increased the rate of their fire.

Brooke meanwhile opened fire at the men across the street from her. She'd taken cover behind a red Fiat, and the bullets from their automatic weapons were punching holes in it everywhere.

One of the shooters cried out and fell, clutching his leg. He tried to drag himself behind a vehicle but before he could, Brooke shot him again. He stopped moving.

Mark, meanwhile, was still crouched behind the front of the vehicle he'd landed behind, placing the engine block between himself and his attackers. A round snapped close over head and another ricocheted beneath the car. He stuck his hand up with the P30 in it and fired blindly, blowing off half the magazine.

Then something strange happened. From the back of their SUV a volley of shots erupted and the second shooter who was firing at Brooke fell next to his friend.

Brooke heard a savage outburst of Italian spew forth which amounted to the Italian version of, "Fuck you, asshole!"

Brooke glanced at Mark who looked just as surprised. He shrugged and mouthed WTF?

Brooke turned her attention to the two remaining shooters who had Mark in their sights. By now they realized that they had lost the advantage and were under fire from three different angles.

So, they ran.

"They're squirting!" Mark called out.

"Let them go."

Brooke moved across the street to the two dead shooters. She took out her cell and captured photos. "Come on, let's go."

They ran back to the SUV and climbed in. Mark turned in the front seat and looked at Isabella. "What was that?"

"They shot at me."

"Where the hell did you get a gun?"

"From Grace. She's been training me to use it since she got there."

"And getting results as well," Mark said with a grin.

Brooke put the SUV into gear and said, "Let's get out of here."

———

Grace called later that evening while they were eating spaghetti. "The guys that hit you were Mafia."

"Why would Mafia be after us?" Brooke asked.

"You'll need to ask them that one," Grace said.

"Anything else?"

"Nothing."

"Is Werner there?" Brooke asked.

"I'll just get him."

A few moments later, Werner came on. "What can I do for you?"

"What can you tell me about Mirabella Bay? The village and the place."

"It's not there anymore," he replied.

"I know that. What else?"

"It was destroyed in World War Two. Up until then it was the better part of a thousand years old. It used to be a trading port for the region. Lots of activity and history."

"What about the monastery?"

"Wait a moment."

There was a drawn-out silence before he said, "Brothers of the Cross. Again, centuries old. It was said that they used to give refuge to pirates and travelers alike. Why?"

"Not sure. What can you tell me about Father Ignatius?"

"That, my dear, is not up my alley. Talk to Grace."

Grace came back on. "What is it?"

Brooke said, "Father Ignatius. Tell me what you know."

"He's been at the church the longest. Before then he was at the monastery."

Brooke said, "That's pretty thin."

Grace said, "So is his life. It's like he didn't exist before then. On the other hand, the cross was a good find. We're all still trying to figure out if there are more things at the church that are on the disappeared list."

"Copy."

The call disconnected. Brooke turned to Mark. "We'll head up to the Bay tomorrow."

"Not me," Bella replied. "I have something else I need to do."

"What?" Brooke asked.

"I'm going to see the Capozzis."

"I'm not sure that is a good idea, Bella," Brooke said.

"I'll be fine. They won't hurt me. They would be too scared of retribution."

"They didn't seem to worry about that earlier," Mark pointed out.

"They didn't know who I was."

"Just be careful."

"Yes, ma'am."

———

Rome, Italy

"Five minutes to interdiction," Carmen said as she waited in the shadows for the scientist's Mercedes to come along the darkened street.

"Copy," Cosimo replied.

"Roger," replied Marco.

Cosimo was in charge of the second team while the first was commanded by Carmen. Marco had a suppressed sniper rifle in an elevated position where he could disable the target vehicle. That would enable the two teams to swoop in and scoop up the scientist.

Once in their custody, they would hook up with the helicopter and get out of Rome. Smooth, easy, no problems.

"Two minutes."

"I have the vehicle in sight," Marco said.

"Get ready."

"Carmen, we may have a problem. I count two escort vehicles."

Carmen thought for a moment. Then she said, "The guy is a nuclear scientist. With what he knows they won't let him travel alone."

What she actually thought was that the intel she'd been given about the target was all fucked up. Her father's people were doing things half-assed again. *Christ!*

"Stand by, Marco."

She waited another minute making sure everything was fine.

"I need the all-clear, Carmen," Marco said in a low voice.

"Teams ready?"

"Yes, boss."

"Marco, send it."

The sniper rifle kicked back against his shoulder and the SUV with the scientist inside came to a sudden stop. Meanwhile the two ground teams with their suppressed Heckler and Koch G36Cs emerged from their hides and took out the escort vehicles.

The lead vehicle turned suddenly right and crashed into a streetlamp. It crunched to a halt and three guards climbed out and walked into a hailstorm of fury. They cried out under the impact of the rounds which assaulted them, and fell to the pavement.

Meanwhile, Carmen's team concentrated on the second escort SUV. They fired round after round until the SUV came to a shuddering stop. The two surviving shooters on the inside piled out. Both took two steps and were mowed down by Carmen's crew.

Carmen used hand signals to get her team to move forward to the second SUV. The first one to reach it opened the door and then the second dragged the scientist from the rear seat. With his hands up as high as he could get them while being reefed from his sanctuary, he beseeched them not to shoot him. They stood him on the road, tied his hands and blindfolded him and then put him in the rear of a van driven by another team member.

It was over in under two minutes. The attackers disappeared into the Rome night, leaving a scene of carnage and destruction behind them.

———

"Shall we intervene?" the solidly built man asked as they watched the events unfold. His accent was thick: German.

Anika Meyer shook her head. "No."

"What do we do then?" he asked.

"I will let Mister Stuber know and he can make that decision."

"The man is a nuclear scientist."

"I know, Walther."

"Do we follow?"

"Yes. But I do not want to be compromised. Where are our friends?"

"Still in Sicily."

Anika nodded. "Put a team on Carmen. We will go there."

————

The sat phone rang just as Anika was about to board the Bombardier Global 7500 business jet for Sicily. She hit the answer button and said, "Yes?"

"Why are you in Rome?" Kurt Stuber asked his enforcer.

"I followed Carmen and her people here," she replied.

"Why? They are not the ones you should be occupied with." His voice was abrupt. "You have other things to worry about."

"They kidnapped a nuclear scientist," Anika explained. "It just confirms that they have the material."

"Not our problem, Anika."

"It will be if they detonate it. It will be everyone's problem," she pointed out sharply.

"Ortega would not be so stupid," Stuber growled.

"Ortega?"

"Yes, Father Juan Ortega."

"Damn it, Kurt, what else aren't you telling me? Don't you think I should have known what I was dealing with?"

"That's just it, Anika, you are not dealing with it."

"I will not stand by and watch him kill thousands of people. This affects us all, Kurt."

Stuber went quiet. Then, "I hear you have been sleeping with the enemy."

"It seemed like a way to get information from him."

"Has it yielded anything?"

"Not yet."

"Is this going to affect anything when the time comes to kill him, Anika?" Stuber asked.

"No."

"Fine. Get back to Sicily."

"That is where we're headed."

The call ended.

9

DANGER EVERYWHERE

Mirabella Bay

The water of Mirabella Bay was 95% clear, apart from the occasional cloud of sediment that wafted from the bottom of the Bay itself. Brooke and Mark drifted lazily along the bottom, trying to find anything that might indicate the past presence of the ships. Fish swam lazily past, drifting amongst patches of coral and rock. It was a peaceful, tranquil scene.

They had arrived about an hour earlier, changed into their wetsuits and put on their scuba tanks. The town itself was in the background. Piles of rubble, broken walls, and mostly destroyed sandstone buildings.

The monastery was set up a little further along the coast, watching over the Bay itself like a giant sentinel. It made Mark wonder how it had survived the Second World War when the village itself had been destroyed. Then he just stared at it, taking in its magnificence.

"It's wonderful, isn't it?" Brooke said.

Mark nodded. "And then some."

He was about to turn away and finish getting ready

for the dive when he caught a flash of sunlight off something shiny. He paused and stared back up on the ridges. "Did you see that?"

Brooke frowned. "See what?"

"I caught a flash of sunlight off something up near the monastery."

"Could have been anything."

"Yeah, you're right."

Once they were ready, they slipped into the water. It was almost warm, soothing, and welcoming. Beneath the surface was beautiful.

They sifted through the silt on the bottom of the bay. Swam in and out of the masses of coral, past the fish.

A Mediterranean Moray or a Roman eel, as it was known, poked its head out of its hole and watched Brooke slowly swim past. Its body was as thick as her arm. Once she was gone, it slipped back into its hole.

They came across a large sandy place on the bottom. Mark started to fluff around with the sand and silt. Then he stopped when something caught his eye. He reached down and picked it up, holding it so he could get a closer look at it. At first, he didn't know what it was. Then it came to him. It was pottery. He showed Brooke before placing it into the bag he had tied to his waist.

Mark and Brooke continued to sift through the silt on the bottom of the Bay in that one area. Next thing he found looked like a bronze ring. He held it up for Brooke to see, and she nodded.

She found the next item. It looked to be an old coin. Slowly they added to their collection of things in the bag. There was nothing really convincing in the signs that the great treasure ship had once been there.

Mark reached out and grabbed Brooke by the arm. She looked at him, and he pointed across at the other side of the large sand base they were searching. At first, she wondered what he was pointing at, and she saw it. A black tip shark swam lazily in circles watching them, trying to decide if they were food or friend.

They watched it for a moment and then it swam away. Keeping a cautious eye in the shark's direction, they returned to their search, finding more rings and pottery.

Brooke tapped Mark on the arm. He looked at her and she pointed towards the surface. The pair swam up and broke through into the clear day. Brooke removed the regulator from her mouth and said, "There is nothing here."

Mark nodded. "I agree."

"You know what that means, don't you?"

"The treasure was offloaded before the ships were burned."

"It had to be. The question is, where was it taken?"

Mark looked up at the monastery and saw the flash again. "Someone is still watching what we're doing."

"Maybe they're just curious," Brooke said.

"Maybe."

"Come on, let's get out."

They were about to swim back when Mark noticed a line of air bubbles coming towards them. "We've got company, Brooke."

"Go under," she snapped.

The pair went back down and could see in the distance two divers coming towards them. It was possible the newcomers were friendly, but Brooke was picking up a menacing vibe from them. It might have had something to do with the spearguns.

Brooke pointed at the coral beds below. Mark nodded and drew his knife, swimming down. The coral beds were large enough to provide cover from the intruders, however, the line of air bubbles rising from their regulators was a proverbial neon arrow to their position.

Mark swam wide in a circle, trying to come up behind the other divers. Brook, on the other hand, found an open-ended cave. With a couple of swift kicks, she was inside and out of sight.

She grabbed her own knife and waited.

Mark's circling seemed to work, and he moved slowly along the bottom, stalking the divers as though he was a shallow-sea predator. The divers stopped and one of them pointed to a line of bubbles rising to the surface. With hand signals he indicated that they would split up.

Their first mistake. And their worst.

Mark picked his target and closed the gap from beneath and behind. By the time the diver felt something was wrong, Mark was upon him.

The diver twisted and tried to bring the speargun around to fire. Mark blocked the weapon and thrust the knife forward, the blade slicing through the man's wetsuit and into the flesh beneath.

The wounded man let out a cry of pain which was garbled by the water. Mark withdrew the knife, a cloud of blood creating a red mist in the clear blue water.

Mark thrust the knife once more, this time sliding it between ribs, finding the diver's heart. The fatally wounded man hunched over, spasmed and then became limp amid a growing cloud of blood.

With a shove, Mark pushed him towards the sea floor, the man's weight belt taking him lower. Free of his attacker, Mark looked around for the other diver who was hunting Brooke.

Brooke was still hiding in the cave, waiting amongst the fish that had come to investigate their own intruder. She held her knife in a tight grip, pointed forward.

It wasn't long before she sensed the danger, a distur-bance in the current washing through the tunnel. Turn-ing, she saw the diver coming in from the other end.

She'd been complacent in her vigilance. She rolled to a sitting position, kicking her feet to propel herself back.

The diver brought up the speargun to fire, but mother nature intervened with perfect timing. Just as the diver was about to fire, a large, thick moray thrust itself out of its hole knocking the speargun aside. The diver pulled the trigger at the same time and the spear sliced through the water past Brooke's shoulder.

She kicked furiously and shot out of the cave, turning back to see the diver coming after her. Swimming to meet him, the two became locked in a desperate death struggle.

The man was strong and turned Brooke's wrist so that she was forced to drop the knife. It fell slowly through the water towards the ocean bed. The diver's other hand grabbed at Brooke's mask as he tried to rip it from her face. She tried to hit him with her fist, but the water made her blows useless.

With his grip still on her mask, the diver managed to pull it forward, admitting a rush of seawater. He then grabbed at her regulator as she struggled to break free, and the diver tore it from her mouth.

Now she couldn't see or breathe.

It was only a matter of moments before panic set in. Through the exertions of the tussle, her body craved air, her lungs beginning to burn. Sudden realization sank in that Brooke was about to drown and there wasn't much she could do about it.

"Fuck you!" she screamed, and a burst of bubbles burst forward from her mouth.

But then her attacker stiffened and went limp. Brooke was confused until Mark appeared and she saw the spear in the sinking body.

She grabbed the regulator and pushed it back into her mouth, taking in a lungful of life-giving air. Mark signaled for them to head up. When they broke the surface into the Mediterranean sunlight, Brooke gasped and said, "Thank you."

"You had him covered."

"Not hardly. Who do you figure they were?"

"No idea. But I think someone does."

When they reached the shore, they climbed out onto the beach and then up the rocky shoreline to where the SUV was parked. The pair changed back into their normal clothes and Brooke ran the towel through her hair before throwing it over to Mark. "Here."

He did the same. "What do we do now?"

Brooke stared at him. "I think we should go back and talk to Father Ignatius. I get the inkling he's our man."

"Do you think he's hiding something?" Mark asked.

"I'm almost certain of it."

———

Isabella paid the fare before climbing out of the taxi. She stood on the cobbled street staring at the sign for a café above her as the vehicle sped away. Stepping up onto the pavement, she pushed open the door to the premises. A small bell jingled, signaling her entrance.

A middle-aged woman looked up from what she was doing at the counter. "Can I help you?" she asked in Italian.

"I am looking for Enzo," Isabella replied.

The woman stared at her suspiciously. "I do not know an Enzo."

"I'm quite sure you do. Tell him Giovanni's daughter is here to see him."

Once more, the woman stared at her through grey eyes, assessing the veracity of Isabella's words. For a moment, Isabella thought that she might not do anything.

Then she turned and went out through the curtain into the back.

Isabella looked around the small cafe. There were four patrons inside. Two were larger men wearing suits sitting against the wall beneath a mirror. And two were older men with a chess board between them, sitting in the corner, drinking coffee, and playing their game.

Not long after the woman reappeared, she said, "Follow me out the back."

Isabella did the woman's bidding, entering a kitchen which was reminiscent of the one her mother had cooked in when Isabella was just a child. A man stood kneading pizza dough at an island. He appeared to be about fifty, had a graying mustache which matched his hair. He looked up at Isabella and said, "What can I do for the daughter of Giovanni Pavesi?"

"You can call your people off my friends," Isabella said, staring him in the eye.

The mafia boss stopped what he was doing and met her gaze. "What are you talking about?"

"Yesterday when we left the church. Your people attacked us. We killed two of them."

"You were with them?"

"Yes."

His expression gave nothing away. "I didn't know."

"Now you do."

"Then we have a problem," Enzo said.

"Not one I would like to have," Isabella said holding his stare.

"I have given my word that these people would be taken care of."

"Your words to pirates?" Isabella said. "What about the code? I'm sure my father would happily remind you of it."

"You do not understand," Enzo replied dismissively as he went back to work on the pizza.

"Try me, Mister Capozzi."

He stopped again. "Even your father would not cross these people. He knows better."

"Mister Capozzi, if this continues, there will be a war."

"You do not have enough people."

"I came here as a friend, Mister Capozzi. I would like to leave that way."

Enzo nodded. "So be it."

"Thank you."

———

"Hello, Father," Brooke said to Ignatius, startling him.

"Y—you are back," he stammered.

"Yes, we need to ask you some more questions," Mark said.

"Yes?"

"We had a dive at the bay and there was nothing there," Brooke explained. "We met some really nasty people, and someone was watching us."

"R—really?"

"Yes, really."

"Oh, dear."

"Who were they?"

"I—I don't know."

"Can you tell us what happened to the crew?" Mark asked changing his line of questioning, figuring Ignatius was too scared to tell them anything.

"I told you they were taken to the monastery."

"What happened after that?"

"You shouldn't be here," Ignatius said. "Not after what happened."

He scratched his arm nervously. Mark frowned.

"What happened to them, Father?" Brooke asked.

"They—they died. That's it, I remember now, they died."

"Would the monastery have records, Father?"

"Yes."

"Fine, we will go there."

"If I were you, I would stay away from the monastery," Ignatius warned them.

"Why?" Brooke asked.

"It is not a place to be."

They left Father Ignatius in the church and once they were outside, Mark said, "He's got a tattoo."

"What?"

"When he scratched his arm, I saw the tattoo. He's part of the Order."

"Great. They'll know what we're up to."

"Do you still want to go to the monastery?" Mark asked.

Brooke nodded. "Yes. We'll do it tomorrow. I'm interested in finding out how Bella got on."

———

Isabella waved down a white taxi and climbed in. So deep in thought, she wasn't aware of her surroundings as the driver took her through the narrow streets. It wasn't until she climbed out that Isabella knew she was in trouble. After the driver had driven away, she looked around for the hotel. When she couldn't see it, she knew that the driver had not dropped her anywhere near it.

"Cazzo!" she hissed vehemently. "Shit."

She glanced around hurriedly and the first thing that hit her was just how silent and dead the street was. Then the car appeared. Dark, with tinted windows, moving slowly. And she didn't have a gun. She'd left it to go and visit Enzo Capozzi. Her father always said, 'there was no point in talking peace when you are loaded for war'.

Walking away from the vehicle that was rolling slowly, creeping up behind her, Isabella was scared but not like she would have been before. Grace had taught her a lot, even in the short time she had been there.

Rely on your friends. They will help you.

Isabella reached for her cell. She hit the speed dial and it was answered by Brooke. "Hey, kid, what's up?"

"I'm in trouble."

The tone of Brooke's voice changed. "Talk to me."

She gave Brooke a fast rundown of what was happening.

"Where are you?"

"I'm not sure."

Tires screeched and a second vehicle appeared in front of her. It came towards her, faster than the other.

Brooke said, "Hide your cell on you so we can track it."

"Listen, it has to be Enzo Capozzi. He is scared of the Order. If you need help, go to my father."

"We're not going to lose you, Bella."

Suddenly it all became too much for her. "I'm worried, Brooke."

"Hang in there."

Isabella tucked the cell into her pants and watched as the second vehicle stopped in front of her. The two rear doors opened and armed men climbed out. She gave them her best smile and said, "I think I'm lost."

———

Brooke found Isabella's cell on the street where she'd been taken. Whoever had kidnapped Isabella had searched her before they'd put her in the back of the vehicle. Mark said, "She could be anywhere."

Brooke looked helplessly around the street. An unseen dog barked a low, hollow sound. "She told us who was responsible. I doubt they will do anything to hurt her. They will use her to lure us in."

"So, we give them what they want," Mark said.

Brooke nodded. "Yes, but we prepare first."

She took out her cell, searching for a number before dialing it, waiting for the voice on the other end. "We have a problem. I need your help."

Once Brooke disconnected the call, she turned to Mark. "I've been given an address and a time tonight."

"Where?" asked Mark.

"On the outside of town."

They climbed back into the SUV and Brooke started it. She was about to put it into gear when an elderly man appeared at her window. It startled her at first but once she recovered, she wound down her window and said, "Can I help you?"

"You look for the girl?" he asked in Italian.

"Yes. Did you see what happened?"

"The men took her. Two."

"Two men?"

"No, auto."

"Cars?"

"Yes," he replied nodding vigorously.

"Do you know who they were?" Mark asked.

"Yes. Bad men."

"Bad men?"

"Yes."

"What bad men?" Brooke asked.

"Very bad."

"Capozzi?"

"Yes."

Brooke nodded. "Thank you."

She disengaged the park brake and by the time she looked back the man had vanished.

———

Isabella stared at Enzo Capozzi. "You have made a mistake, Mister Capozzi. My father will not let this go."

The mafia man looked nervous for a someone with his power. "You do not understand."

"That's what you said last time." Isabella looked around the study of the Mafia man's elaborate home. "My father—"

"Your father will do nothing," Capozzi snarled. "He will not go against the Order."

"You sound so confident."

"That is because I know what I'm talking about."

"Even if what you say is true, my people will not stand by."

Capozzi nodded. "That is what I am counting on."

After they had taken Isabella off the street, they had brought her here to the villa. She had been locked away in a room until now when summoned before the mafia don. "It will not be as easy as you think."

Capozzi had heard enough. He waved her away. "Lock her back in the room and then increase security."

"Yes, sir," said one of the two large men who stood either side of Isabella.

The mafia don watched them escort her out and hoped that she was wrong.

———

Brooke and Mark sat waiting in the SUV, parked in a warehouse parking lot. It was after dark, and still there was no sign of those they were supposed to meet. "They're late," Mark said.

"These are people you do not rush," Brooke replied.

"You would think that considering the circumstances a hint of urgency might be required."

"They won't hurt her," Brooke reiterated.

Headlights appeared. Four of them—two vehicles. One sedan, the other an SUV. They eased to a stop and men emerged. One from the sedan's front passenger seat, opened the rear door for the occupant to alight.

A woman.

In her late forties. She wore long pants and a suit jacket over which her dark hair hung to the shoulders. She stepped forward, hips swaying as though a model walking down a Milan runway.

Brooke and Mark followed their lead and climbed out as well. The woman stopped in front of them, illuminated by the vehicles' headlights. "Hello, Brooke."

"Hello, Mia."

"Giovanni couldn't come but I have what you need."

"Couldn't? Or wouldn't?" Brooke asked Isabella's mother.

She shrugged. "You know how he is." She looked at Mark. "Who is this handsome man?"

"He's not for you," Brooke replied. "His name is Mark."

Mia pouted. "It is a pity. I have heard Bella talk of him. He is...mmm."

"Why do I feel like a piece of meat all of a sudden?" Mark asked.

"If you are the meat then I would surely chew on it," Mia replied.

"Focus, Mia."

"I am just having some fun. I like the way he squirms. The weapons are in the other vehicle."

They moved to the rear of the SUV and the back was opened. Inside they found tactical vests and weapons. Beretta ARX160s complete with suppressors and spare magazines. "Any NVGs?" Mark asked.

"They are there, too."

"Where did you get all this?"

Mia shrugged. "As an organization, we have to adapt."

"Fine. Now, where will we find Enzo?"

Mia held out her hand and one of her men passed over a file. "Everything you need will be in there."

Brooke took it and said, "Thank you."

"Just make sure you get my daughter back. Nothing should happen to her."

"That's the plan."

Mia stared at them and nodded. Then she walked towards the vehicle she had arrived in. About to climb in, she turned and said, "Make sure you kill Enzo. Even in the mafia we have rules."

———

They planned their assault on the fly. The aerial photos supplied by Mia Mandela Pavesi were marked with positions of guards and cameras. Although not complete, it gave Brooke and Mark an idea of what they were up against.

The weapons were double checked, and they went through the plan once more. Brooke said, "We take out the sentries and then enter, clearing the ground floor. Bella will most likely be upstairs."

"Once we reach the second floor then we start clearing each room. If we find her before we finish clearing, we get out as fast as we can."

"What if she isn't on either?" Mark asked.

"Then we check the basement."

"Wouldn't it be the obvious place to check?" Mark said.

"That's possibly what Enzo is thinking too."

Mark shook his head. "Man, I thought this was all behind me when I got out."

"Are you alright?"

"I'm good."

"Then, let's do this."

After climbing from their SUV, they cut their way through the perimeter fence. They took root in a garden bed for a few minutes to watch the sentries. Then with their suppressed ARX 160s raised, they moved.

From the shrubs they broke cover, Brooke taking point. Immediately she engaged the first guard. Three shots from her weapon put the surprised man down on the damp grass.

They moved on, Brooke taking them left. A second shadow emerged, and he too joined his friend in the promised land.

Beside a small bush, Brooke stopped and checked the feed on her display which was running from Webster's terminal in Berlin. He'd hacked into a satellite feed and was bouncing the signal back to Brooke.

Touching the screen, she found the other sentries. She looked at Mark and used hand signals to indicate which direction she wanted him to go.

With Mark taking point, they went right towards a large outdoor entertainment area. Keeping low and to the shadows, he climbed some sandstone stairs and as he crested them, shot the next sentry by the pool.

The guard cried out before falling into the pool with a splash. Mark stopped and waited to see whether the sudden noise elicited any kind of reaction.

As he waited, Mark could feel the coolness of the

night. He swept the area, the laser sight looking like a green lance that reached out through the green haze of the NVGs. When no one appeared, Brooke touched his shoulder.

Mark moved again. Around the pool the water was already changing color, the blood draining from the corpse floating in it. He cut through an evergreen hedge and turned the corner of the building.

The interior was illuminated, but curtains blocked excess light from escaping. According to the house's blueprints, there was a side door which Mark now made for. He also knew that the mafia don lived there with his wife.

They caught the last sentry and Mark ended the man's evening with three well-placed rounds. Then he turned his attention to the side door.

"Wait," Brooke whispered.

She checked her ISR feed. "It's clear."

Mark tried the door and found it unlocked.

Pushing it open cautiously, he stepped to the side before entering the room.

The rattle of automatic fire filled the house and bullets chewed furrows in the door frame. Mark dropped to his knees, swore, and opened fire at a figure holding a weapon. The shooter fell backward with three bullets in his chest.

Brooke moved past Mark, her weapon up. "Well, they know we're here."

"I think they already knew."

Mark pressed forward, moving from the entryway into a long hallway. He cleared right, and then swept left. Another shooter appeared and died.

"You go right, I'll go left," Mark said going against everything that made sense. Splitting their force to clear the ground floor against so many unknowns was crazy.

"Copy," Brooke replied.

The hallway opened out into a foyer, off which there were four doorways. A shooter appeared from the one to the left. Her suppressed ARX 160 hammered twice, and the man died.

Brooke pushed towards the opening from which he had emerged. She checked with a glance and entered. The room, a large living area, was empty.

Stepping over the body on the floor, she walked back into the foyer. Brooke moved to the second doorway and cleared that room, then the next. She'd just emerged when she felt the barrel of a handgun pressed against the left side of her head. "Put the gun down, signorina."

Brooke let the weapon go so it hung by its strap, and raised her hands. "Fuck."

She stood rock still, her right hand dangling near the holstered P30 on her right thigh out of sight. "What now?" she asked.

"Now we—"

Brooke used the minor distraction to make her move. She grabbed the P30, turned so the muzzle of the Italian's weapon disengaged from her head and drove her own weapon into his stomach before firing five rounds into his torso.

The man grunted in surprise; his eyes wide as he sank to his knees. Brooke placed the P30 against his forehead and fired a sixth round, blowing his brains across the polished tile floor.

She quickly holstered the handgun before taking the ARX back up. It was then that another shooter appeared at the head of the stairs and opened fire.

———

Mark eased his way into a large media room with his suppressed ARX up on his shoulder, ready to fire. Three walls were a dark color, the end one white for the projector. There were three rows of lounge chairs, leather with cupholders, facing the white wall where a movie would play.

He eased his way around the leather chairs when a shooter suddenly appeared. The man was just as surprised as Mark, but it was the latter who recovered first.

The ARX fired and the new arrival collapsed to the floor, blood pooling around him. Mark hurried over to where the dead man lay and kicked the weapon out of reach just to be safe.

Mark kept moving. *Treasure hunting should never be this dangerous*, he thought.

Inside an adjoining room was another pool, a heated indoor one. The smell of chlorine was thick in the air, along with the humidity.

Another armed guard appeared. He opened fire hastily and sprayed the wall near Mark, who returned fire. The man lurched back, bullets in his chest, his finger depressing the trigger reflexively.

Bullets drove skyward, shattering the glass ceiling so that razor sharp shards rained down like sheets of ice.

Then Mark heard gunfire coming from the other direction. He turned and hurried in that direction, knowing that Brooke would be in trouble.

By the time he reached the foyer, Brooke had taken cover behind a short pillar topped with a bust of Julius Caesar. However, due to the fusillade of bullets hitting it, the structure was slowly disintegrating.

Mark brought his ARX up, searching for a target. "Where is he?"

"Top of the stairs, left post."

"Got it."

Mark stepped away from cover, walking to his right. Then he saw the shooter. The sights came on and he fired. Missed, and fired again.

The shooter died.

Brooke came to her feet. "Thanks."

"You've made a habit of getting into sticky situations lately."

"Get your ass up the stairs."

Their boots sounded loud on the polished wood as they ascended. Reaching the landing, Mark shot the downed shooter who made a noise as they went past. The change in him was noticeable.

People trying to kill you would do that.

They reached the first door and Mark opened it. The room was clear. Along the hallway were three more doors. Brooke touched his shoulder. "Follow me."

She skipped the second door and stopped outside of the third. She raised the ARX and nodded to Mark who opened the door.

Gunfire rattled from inside, but Brooke held firm and put the shooter down. She then shifted her aim to cover the man holding a handgun to Isabella's head. "Put it down" Brooke said firmly.

In the low lamplight the man looked determined to hold firm. "No, you put yours down."

"Not going to happen," Brooke replied as Mark moved in beside her.

"You OK, kid?" Mark asked.

"Yes."

Brooke said, "I'm going to count to three and if you haven't put the weapon down, we know what happens next."

Capozzi said, "I have the upper—"

THWAP! THWAP!

Brooke fired twice, both rounds hitting the mafia man in the head. He fell back and landed on the floor with a dull thud. "Get her untied, Mark. It's time to go."

———

Sicily

Carmen walked into her father's hall and found him sitting alone on his chair. The clock on the wall had just chimed one. He looked to be deep in thought and then she saw he was looking at something. When he saw her approach, he turned whatever it was face down on the table.

"You are back. Where is my scientist?"

"He was taken down to the chamber."

"Good, was there any trouble?"

Carmen shook her head. "No, father."

"Good." He stared at her silently and she knew there was more. "Our friends have been around. They were diving down at the old wreck site. I sent some men to scare them away?"

"And?"

"They did not return."

"You should have left them be."

"You should have already gotten rid of them," he hissed. "They are a threat to the Order."

"You mean a threat to whatever it is you are doing. What is it, by the way?"

"You do not need to know." He paused. "They went and saw Ignatius. I want him gone."

"He is a loyal follower, father," Carmen pointed out.

"He knows too much."

"He is too scared to go against us."

"Kill him, Carmen. It is a command."

"Yes, father." Her words were acidic. "I will obey."

She turned and walked towards the large wooden doors. As she reached out to open one of them, her father said, "Do it tonight."

The door boomed close behind her.

———

There was a light knock on their door early the following morning and the three of them looked at each other. Mark picked up his handgun and walked towards the entry. Brooke followed suit and picked up her own, waving Isabella away from the center of the room.

Brooke nodded as she raised hers and pointed it at the doorway. Mark opened the door and revealed Anika standing there with a paper in her hand.

"They kidnapped a nuclear scientist from Rome and brought him here to Sicily," she said as she entered their room. She dropped the paper on the table and continued, "They also killed Father Ignatius."

"What the hell are you doing here?" Brooke demanded.

"I need your help."

Brooke's eyebrows shot up. "What?"

"To stop them from whatever they are doing."

"Why don't you just go to Interpol?" Mark asked.

"You might make wonderful love, Mark, but you are such a child."

"Why do you need our help, Anika?"

"Because Kurt has other things on his mind and doesn't see the threat that I do."

"You want us to help stop whatever is happening?" asked Brooke.

Anika nodded. "Yes."

"Why would we do that?" Isabella asked.

"Because if it can't be stopped, I am certain the Order will detonate the world's largest dirty bomb and screw it up for thousands of years. I may be an assassin, but I am not a psychopath."

"But why would they do that?"

"Who knows? There has to be a reason," Anika said. "Maybe if we find out the 'why' we find out the 'where'."

Brooke looked at Anika. "How many people do you have?"

"I have a small team."

"We need to know who we're dealing with and that we can trust you."

Anika nodded. "You can. The truth lies within the monastery."

"The monastery?" Mark asked.

"Yes. The bishop's name is Ortega."

"Ortega? As in Captain Esteban Ortega?"

Anika nodded. "Yes, Father Juan Ortega. He is the leader of the Order. Carmen is his daughter."

Brooke stared at Anika. "What else do you know?"

"Not a lot. Kurt was holding out on me."

10

THE RED DEATH

The Atlantic, 1672

The deck of the *Golden Hawk* was awash with blood. Spars from aloft had crashed to the deck under the onslaught of Captain Esteban Ortega's guns from his more maneuverable galleon. It hadn't taken them long to find then attack the galleon.

Many men had died violent deaths. First under the roar of cannon shot, and the tearing of wooden splinters. Then Ortega had come alongside the galleon and sent his men over the side to board her.

Now, with the *Golden Hawk* under his control, Ortega had moved onto the next part of his plan. Before him stood Bishop Torres and Alejandro Garza, the latter with a bitter expression on his face. "You are a dog, Esteban," he growled as he cradled his right arm. It was broken when a spar had fallen from aloft and caught him a glancing blow.

Ortega stared at him through narrow eyes. Before joining the Spanish Navy, Ortega had grown up on the streets, an urchin who begged, borrowed, and stole to survive. He had even killed. Until one day he had been found by a man with a special tattoo on his arm. Or rather, Ortega had found him in a market and tried to pick his pocket. The man's name was Abad Fernandez, and he had caught Ortega in the act. Instead of turning him over to have justice meted out upon him, he'd taken him home to his rather fancy house and fed him fancy food.

The tattoo was the mark of the Spanish Order. And Fernandez was unlike any he had known before. He was a ship's captain and had taken Ortega to sea, teaching him everything he knew.

For the next four years Fernandez showed Ortega all there was to know about captaining a ship. From reading charts, navigation, and commanding men, and life in the rigging. But most of all, he taught Ortega about being a privateer, in those days, another word for a pirate.

Then one day they had been caught by a British Fifth Rate ship, much like a frigate, of 36 guns. Battle was joined during which Fernandez had been killed. Ortega took command and the *Albatross* carried the day.

Then upon returning to port, Ortega left the ship to join the Spanish Navy. Now, here he was about to steal one of the largest treasures ever transported across the ocean. All in the name of the Spanish Order.

"You will burn in hell for this," Torres growled.

Ortega smiled. "Perhaps I will see you there, Bishop Torres. I have heard all about your ways and I'm sure you shall be there before me."

"Damn you," Torres snarled. "Damn you in the eyes of God."

Ortega looked to one of his men. He gave a curt nod, and the man came forward, wrapping a rope around the bishop's neck and tying it off. When he was done, the other end was fixed to a bag with a cannon ball inside. The man then waited for Ortega to give the next order.

Another nod and two men dragged the struggling Torres to the side of the *Golden Hawk*. Once they reached the rail, Ortega said, "Do you have any last words?"

The bishop stared at him defiantly.

Ortega said, "Throw him over."

And moments later, Torres disappeared screaming over the side.

"You are an animal, Esteban," Garza snarled.

Ortega drew his flintlock handgun and cocked it, then without a word he shot the captain in the head.

"Get them all over the side. Cut their throats as you do it. Then we will leave. I will be in the captain's cabin."

As he walked past one of his men, he could see that the man was looking pale and sweating. Ortega stopped and said, "Are you alright?"

The man nodded. "I am fine, Captain."

Ortega nodded and walked on.

———

Algiers, 1672

There were dead below decks on both ships. The sickness had swept through both vessels and killed most of those they touched. Ortega climbed over the side of the *Golden Hawk* and rowed towards the shore with some of his crew who weren't sick.

They pulled up beside a long wharf and he climbed out under the watchful eye of four armed men. "Who are you?" one of them asked.

"I am Captain Esteban Ortega. I am looking for a doctor."

"Why would that be?"

"Because some of my crew are sick."

"Do they have the Red Death?" The man who asked the question was concerned.

The Red Death referred to the victim coughing blood in the latter stages before death. "No," Ortega lied.

The man was skeptical. "Wait here, I will fetch a doctor for you."

So, Ortega waited. He went back to the boat and climbed up. "What is happening, Captain?" one of the sailors asked.

"They are fetching a doctor."

"Did you tell them it was the Red Death?"

Ortega's eyes narrowed. "Shut up, you fool, or I will cut out your tongue."

"Sorry, Captain."

An hour elapsed before a doctor came. They took him to the *Golden Hawk* and helped him aboard. Once there it took only moments for his face to pale. "The Red Death is aboard this vessel," he gasped. "What are you doing, man?"

"I need you to make them better," Ortega said.

"Better? I cannot make them better. They are dying. And now by bringing me here you have cursed me too. I cannot leave for fear of spreading it throughout the town. Damn you. I have a wife and children."

"I am sorry, Doctor. Can you at least try?"

"You would be doing them a favor if you cut their throats and burned their bodies in the hope to stop it."

"I will not do that."

"Then you are a bigger fool than I had you figured for."

The doctor's name was Esteban. He was Spanish and a man who would not see anyone suffer while he had a chance to help them. So, he went to work trying to save those he could.

Ortega spent most of the day at the stern of his ship staring out to see. It was late in the afternoon when he heard a shout and turned to see a red rag being run up the main mast. Immediately he knew what it was and who had ordered it. It was a sign that the Red Death was aboard the ship, and it was the work of the doctor.

Ortega turned to one of his men. "Have the doctor brought aft."

"Yes, Captain."

Five minutes later the doctor was standing before him.

"What was the meaning of the flag?" Ortega snapped.

"To warn the town to stay away."

"We need water and food for both ships. How are we to get them now?"

"I cannot help that. My duty is to the people in the town, not to pirates."

Ortega fixed him with an even stare. "So, you know."

"The dying are delirious. They keep asking me to make sure their share goes to friends or family."

Ortega nodded. He turned to the man who'd escorted the doctor to him. "Have the fit muster on deck. We sail before it gets dark. Signal the other ship."

"But to where, Captain?"

"I have no idea."

11

THE MONASTERY

Sicily

The cell buzzed and Brooke answered. It was early the following morning, and she was taking her first coffee in the sun. "Good morning."

"Hey," Grace Cramer said from the other end. "I have something you might be interested in."

"Treasure related?"

"Pirate related."

"Do tell," Brooke said and took another drink.

"It may be nothing but at the moment, even the smallest pieces of information could be gold. Between us all we did some digging and found that the British Navy purged the Med of the pirate curse some five years after the *Golden Hawk* disappeared. What if Ortega was scooped up in their net and hung along with the others?"

"OK, but what are you getting at?"

"I don't know. I was just throwing crap at the wall to see if it would stick."

Brooke thought for a moment as she mulled the information through her mind. Then she had her own idea. "Father Juan Ortega."

"What?"

"The bishop at the monastery here is Father Juan Ortega."

"Oh, shit, really?"

"Yes."

"Where did you find that tidbit of information?"

Assassin. Killer. "Old friend."

"Do you think they could be related?"

"I don't know. We're going to have a look around. My old friend tells me that he is the leader of the Order and that he has a daughter named Carmen."

"And yet, you're still going there," Grace said incredulously.

"I need to know for sure."

"Be careful."

"I'll try."

She disconnected the call and looked at Mark. "Are you ready?"

"I guess so," he replied.

"Me too," said Isabella.

Brooke shook her head. "No, you get on a plane back to Berlin."

"What?"

"Do as I say, Bella, I need to focus all my attention going forward on this. It's too dangerous."

Isabella nodded, understanding the reasoning but sad that her adventure was over. "OK."

———

"We are being watched," Mark said as he opened the door to the SUV.

"I see them," Brooke replied. "They're not being too secretive about it."

Mark drove. He eased away from the curb and started along the cobbled street. Behind them a black BMW did the same. Soon they were on the road to the monastery.

"They're still back there," Mark said.

"Yes, I think I saw our red-headed friend with them."

The monastery loomed in front of them. They passed through large gates and continued along a gravel drive. Mark gave a low whistle. "It's even more impressive close up."

It was a large sandstone building with stained-glass windows, bell tower, and armed guards.

"Weapons under the robes," Brooke said.

"Makes me happy we brought ours," Mark replied. "You thought about how we're going to do this?"

"Consider this as a recon op."

Mark grunted. "One that could get you killed."

He eased the SUV to a halt, and they climbed out. The following BMW rolled up slowly behind them and ceased its movement. Three doors opened. Two men and Carmen climbed out. All were armed. She walked forward and said, "You shouldn't have come here. But it has saved me a job."

"Carmen!"

They looked to the top of the monastery steps and saw a man standing in front of the large wooden, double doors. Carmen gave him a grudging look. "What is it?"

"Your father wants to see the visitors."

"Oh," said Mark. "Daddy calls."

Carmen glared at him, fire in her emerald eyes. "I will bring them in."

"He is in the throne room."

"Give me your weapons."

"Don't have any," Mark said.

Carmen searched them and took their handguns.

"Move," she grunted at them. "And no funny moves or my men will kill you."

The inside of the monastery was grandiose. Gilt ornamental molding surrounded every lead light window and archway, riddled with jewels and precious gems. The floor was marble, and candle holders appeared to be silver. A solid gold cross sat atop the altar. There were other crosses embedded with gems and so much more.

"This way," Carmen said to them.

They walked through an open doorway and found themselves in another room much like the main part of the monastery. Except this one had a large, jeweled throne in it, complete with a man, dressed in robes, seated atop it.

"You wanted to see them, father," Carmen said. "Here they are."

Brooke stared at the man before her. He had a harsh gaze and a dark beard. His hair was neat, and his posture erect. He said, "So, I see, daughter. The question is, what to do with them?"

"If you don't mind, I'd rather not walk the plank," Mark said.

Brooke glared at him.

"Huh, a joker. Why are you here?"

"We came to talk," Brooke replied.

"About what?"

"About the treasure of the *Golden Hawk*."

"What makes you think it is here?" Ortega asked.

"We followed the breadcrumbs," Brooke replied. "We're good at that."

Ortega nodded. "I have heard as much. Your exploits precede you. I would have thought you already had your hands full with Kurt Stuber."

"He's just a teddy bear," Mark replied. "You might even say he's on our side in this."

Ortega's eyes narrowed. "I do not like you. If I were you, I'd keep my mouth shut. Just because you slept with his bitch, does not make him a friend."

Mark rolled his eyes. "Does everyone know?"

Ortega glanced at his daughter. "Take him outside. Show him the view from the clifftop."

"Father—"

"Do it, Carmen. I wish to talk to the woman on her own. She seems to be the only one of sense out of the two of them."

"Yes, father."

She escorted Mark outside, shadowed by Marco. Mark looked over his shoulder and asked, "Does he go everywhere with you?"

"Yes. And if you try anything, he will kill you."

They walked towards the cliff. Down below, waves crashed against the rocks as they had done for millions of years, slowly wearing them away.

"Is this where you push me to my death?" Mark asked.

She gave him a mirthless smile. "Not yet."

"What does your father want with spent nuclear fuel rods?"

If the question surprised her, Carmen didn't let it show. "What fuel rods?"

"The ones off the ship you attacked. The *Venetian Sea*."

"I don't know what you are talking about."

"You realize that if your lot set off a big old dirty bomb, it'll screw things up for thousands of years. Places will be uninhabitable. The whole Mediterranean will be a graveyard. Your graveyard."

Mark wasn't sure but he thought there might have

been a flicker in her eyes. Carman said, "It is a good thing that there is nothing like that going on then, isn't it?"

"Yes, it is." He paused. "Tell me, is it a family business, or like all great parents do, did you get forced into it?"

"Into what?"

"Piracy."

"You don't give up, do you?" Carmen said.

"One day, just not today. Treasure cost my father his life."

Carmen said, "Let's hope the apple doesn't fall too far from the tree."

"As in your case?" Mark asked.

"I am nothing like my father," Carmen hissed losing her composure.

"OK, so you're not your father. So what is he doing with the nuclear material?"

"I do not know."

"And you wouldn't tell me if you did, right?"

"Something like that. And I couldn't tell you that he had a scientist prisoner here as well."

He was about to ask another question when she gave him a work it out yourself look. He just nodded and stared out to sea.

"What to do with you and your friend?" Ortega asked out loud. "I should kill you both but that would cause me more problems. Maybe an accident?"

Brooke just stared at him.

Ortega raised his eyebrows. "No? You and your people are very good at what you do. Very tenacious."

She remained silent.

"You are stubborn like my daughter." He stared at

her. "If you weren't you wouldn't have found the treasure of the Nazis. Tell me, was the Amber Room with it? I heard that it was."

"If you did your research you would know that it was and that Kurt Stuber has it. Except for the Fabergé eggs. Those we have."

Ortega's face became like that of an excited child. "Were they as elegant and as fragile as they look in their pictures?"

"Even more so."

"A shame I cannot see them in person. And now you are here, trying to steal what is mine."

"It is not yours," Brooke said bitterly.

"It has been in our possession for centuries. Who else would you say owns it?"

"Not you."

"I beg to differ. Anyway, it does not matter. I will make a decision about what will happen to you later. Until then, you and your obnoxious friend will be my guests."

———

They were kept in what amounted to a dungeon beneath the monastery. It was cold and damp and uncomfortable. Mark sat with his back against the hard wall while Brooke paced back and forth.

"How's the recon going?" Mark asked sarcastically.

"Shut up," Brooke replied. "I'm thinking."

"Did he tell you anything?"

"No. What about Carmen?"

"She doesn't like her father or what he's doing," Mark said. "If we get half a chance, we might be able to turn her."

"Let's see how things play out," Brooke said. Then, "Did you see it?"

Mark nodded. "I saw it."

The longer they were in there, the colder it became. Then around midnight they were awakened by a deep rumbling sound. The whole monastery felt as though it were shaking.

"Earthquake?" Mark asked.

"Maybe a tremor," Brooke replied.

They waited and after a minute the rumbling stopped. Then through the high window of their prison came the sound of a motor. Brooke looked at Mark. "A boat."

Mark nodded. "This just gets even curiouser."

"Yes, it does."

———

Berlin, Germany

Grace Cramer was reading through electronic files she'd downloaded into a ZIP folder when Molly came looking for her. It was just after midnight. Grace looked up from her work and said, "Hey, shouldn't you be in bed?"

"I could say the same about you," Molly replied.

Grace held up a sheet of paper. "Too much going on."

Molly nodded. "Yes. This whole nuclear thing has me worried. If Ortega is the one who has it, then why does he want it? I was looking through some files and digging as deep as I could and came up with a thread that is so fine it's like gossamer."

"What is it?" Grace asked. "I'll take anything at the moment."

Molly handed her the sheet of paper she'd brought with her. "It seems that back in the day when the British were cleaning out the pirates, they picked up one named Esteban Ariel."

"Who is Esteban Ariel?" Grace asked.

"Look at the part I circled," Molly said.

Grace's eyes flicked over the paper to the part circled in red.

Esteban Ariel Ortega.

She looked up at Molly. "Ortega was picked up by the British in their crackdown on piracy in the Med?"

"I know it's a big net to cast but it's possible."

"Do you have anything else?" Grace asked.

Molly shook her head. "No. There might be records in London but nothing digital."

Grace nodded. "I'll take it to Johann in the morning."

"He's in his office," Molly informed her.

"Then I guess there is no time like the present."

———

Molly's intel was right. Schmidt was at his desk working. He looked up and said, "Can't sleep?"

"I was working when Molly brought me something to look at. I guess the not sleeping thing is going around."

He smiled at her. "How are you settling in?"

"I'm fine. Hit the ground running you might say."

Schmidt touched his sling. "Wish I could say the same. We just hit the ground. Now, what can I do for you, Grace?"

She showed him the piece of paper and the name on it. The billionaire looked at her and said, "I guess you need to go to London to see if you can run it down."

"London?"

He nodded. "Yes, they have a place there called The Hall of Records. Not many people know about it, but if you need answers, then that's where you'll find them."

"Thank you."

"Do you want to take anyone with you?"

Grace shook her head. "I'll be right. Everyone else is busy, anyway."

"Fine. Just be careful. If we've learned anything over the past few months, it's that bad people turn up when you least expect it. I wish Brooke was here, I'd send her with you, but from what she has told me, you can more than look after yourself."

"I will be fine."

————

Sicily

Ortega looked up as Carmen entered the room, and said, "Good morning, daughter."

"Father." Her response was curt, more of a grunt than anything else. "Why do you want me?"

"Johann Schmidt is sending a woman to London to look for things I'd rather not be found. Send one of your people to make sure she doesn't find it. If they are capable."

"I will let our people in London know."

Ortega seemed to nod his approval. "Good. You may leave."

"What are we to do with the ones in the dungeon?"

"Leave them there for the time being."

Carmen left, and soon after that another man entered the room. Olavo. He had a concerned expression on his face. "What is it?" Ortega asked.

"The scientist is saying he doesn't have everything he needs to complete what you want him to do."

"What do you mean?"

"He says that if you want your project completed, he

needs to be working in better conditions. Or not only him, but everyone here will die."

"What does he suggest?"

"He said that before the Curtain came down and the Soviet Union fractured, there was a complex in Romania that could be useful."

Ortega thought for a moment and said, "Yes, all right. Have everything shifted there. You will be in command. Keep me updated."

"Yes, sir."

12

LONDON SECRETS

London, England

Grace flew to Heathrow and from there caught a black cab to a hotel in the city. Just as well Johann was paying for it, for the Royal England was five-hundred pounds a night. She was met at the cab by a man dressed in a black suit, looking more like a butler than a bell hop. "Would madam like her baggage collected?"

"It's only one," Grace told him.

"One too many for an RE customer. Can't have you over doing it when you're on holiday."

"I'm on business actually."

He pulled a face. "Even worse. Head into the desk and I'll be right behind you."

Inside the foyer was another experience. The hotel had gone all out and there were imitation beefeaters standing in various corners. Grace walked up to the desk and was greeted by a young woman of Sri Lankan origin but had the heavy accent of someone from Liverpool. "Can I help you, Miss?"

"I have a room booked under the name of Cramer."

The receptionist clicked on a few computer icons and said, "Yes, here it is. All paid up for a two day stay with the option to extend for an additional two should it be required. I'll have someone show you to your room."

Just over five minutes later she was in her room. Once Grace was settled in, she grabbed her cell and called Brooke. The call rang out and she shrugged. "I'll try later."

Grace looked at her watch. Another hour and it would be dinnertime. The Hall of Records wouldn't be open until eight the following morning. Her cell buzzed and she expected it to be Brooke returning her call, but it wasn't. It was Molly. "Hey up."

"Hi, what's happened?"

"Nothing. Have you talked to Brooke or Mark?"

"No. I tried Brooke not long ago, but she never picked up."

"Me too. Then I tried Mark and he's not answering either."

Grace frowned. "I'm sure it's nothing. I'll try later."

"OK, me too. Say, what's the hotel like?"

Grace said, "I have never stayed in anything like it."

"Johann has a way of picking them."

They talked for a few more minutes and then the call ended. Grace showered and went downstairs to the restaurant. She had a white wine with a lamb dish that tasted like heaven. And the dessert was exquisite.

The night was spent in a large, soft, warm bed and the wakeup call came at 3am.

It was the disturbance in the atmospheric pressure caused by the door opening which brought Grace awake. Her eyes snapped open, and her ears strained to hear what it was that brought her into the land of the living.

Grace's hand slid under the pillow and wrapped

around the grip of the Heckler and Koch P30. Then she waited, listening.

The bedroom itself was separate from the rest of the suite. It was then that she realized that it wasn't the room door that had opened but the bedroom door. Whoever it was, was in there with her. And her back was facing the door.

Grace rolled to bring her P30 into line and made it halfway before it was smashed from her grasp. It hit the floor with a thud and on instinct, Grace rolled away just as a knife came down and buried to its hilt in the mattress.

With a cry of alarm, Grace kicked out, her foot catching the intruder in the face, knocking him back. The blow was solid, and the intruder let go of the knife.

Grace came to her feet and saw the figure on the other side of the bed. A man with broad shoulders.

He launched himself across the bed at Grace figuring his size would be to his advantage. But while Grace wasn't big, she was lithe and quick, and quite proficient in the art of self-defense.

She stood her ground and instead of using a closed fist to hit her attacker in the face, she brought her elbow around and connected solidly with his jaw.

The force of the blow jarred up into Grace's shoulder, but she never backed off. Within a couple of heartbeats, another blow from her elbow and the intruder spilled backwards.

Grace pressed her advantage and threw herself forward across the bed. She bounced off it and came to her feet.

And into a bunched fist that hit her in the jaw. She rocked back on her heels and stars flashed before her eyes. The intruder hit her again in the chest and she staggered back, her legs catching the bed.

As Grace fell back, she twisted and finished on the floor. The man came after her and she caught a glancing blow on her shoulder. Grace grunted and scrambled away from the attacker and came to her feet. Reaching for the bedside lamp, ripping the cord free, Grace flung it at her attacker.

The figure dodged the projected missile and it crashed to the floor, smashing. Grace followed it and landed a flying kick to the intruder's chest. She hit him again, and yet again.

Somehow, she was getting on top of the bigger intruder. Grace lashed out with another bunched fist and her attacker had the instinct to block the blow. Then he hit her in the chest, just under her heart and Grace stopped in her tracks.

The air whooshed from her lungs, and she tried to suck more in, to refill them. Grace's mouth opened and closed like a fish out of water and just as she drew in her first, the intruder hit her again, open handed, knocking her flying.

Grace crashed to the floor and lay there willing herself to rise. The intruder came at her again and grabbed her by the hair. He dragged her to her feet, and she gasped with pain.

Grace lashed out, not willing to give up just yet. She lunged in close, her hands like claws raking the man's face. He gasped as pain burned from the deep scratches.

Grace brought her bunched fist up and he blocked the blow. Then she tried her knee, and before it plunged deep into his crotch, he turned and took the blow on the thigh.

The intruder let out a growl of rage and hit Grace in the stomach, doubling her over. Once more air whooshed from her lungs and she staggered back, this time through the opening of the doorway and out into the suite living area.

The man followed her and shoved Grace brutally backward and she fell over a glass coffee table, crashing through it. She felt a sliver of glass slice into her right thigh and hissed from the pain. The intruder leaned down and dragged her to her knees. In desperation, Grace felt around and grabbed a wicked shard of glass. She swung it with all her strength and felt it go into the man's thigh.

With a cry of pain, the intruder lashed out and hit Grace once more. This time she tasted blood in her mouth.

"Fucking bitch," the attacker growled.

He had a British accent. But he had to be part of the Order. Didn't he?

Grace lurched to her left as she tried to stay out of reach of the intruder. He began to crowd her into a corner. She tried to dive right and then cut back left to wrong foot him but even though he had a deeply lacerated leg, he was still quick enough to stop her.

"Losing a lot of blood?" she sneered. "You'll start getting tired and clumsy soon. Then I'll fucking cut your heart out."

"You will not get the chance," the intruder hissed.

"Bring it, motherfucker," Grace grumbled and the two crashed together as though they were lumbering Sumo wrestlers.

It was time to get serious.

The intruder grabbed at her throat, but Grace pulled free and headbutted him across the nasal bridge. The man reeled back, blood running from his now shattered nose. "Come on, you prick, I'll show you how an Aussie scraps."

With a howl of rage, the intruder rushed forward and wrapped his arms around Grace, trying to squeeze the life from her. With her lungs constricted, Grace struggled to breathe. But she was a fighter and wasn't done yet. Her head came forward and her teeth bit down on his ear. With a savage wrench, the ear parted ways with the intruder's head. Warm blood spurted across Grace's face and the previous howl of pain from the intruder turned into a screech as he released her. Grace staggered back and spat the ear onto the floor, her face looking like Carrie from the Stephen King movie.

She lurched forward, bringing her foot up into the soft underside of his crotch. The attacker dropped to his knees with a grunt. He clutched at his groin and whimpered. But Grace wasn't done. Not just yet. Her final act of pent-up rage was to kick him in the face, breaking his jaw with an audible crack.

She stared down at him, panting hard, and said, "Cop that, asshole."

———

The police questioned Grace for a while before leaving, an escort going to the hospital with the intruder. Grace herself was checked over and her cuts treated by paramedics who attended the scene. She apologized to hotel management about the incident and then called Schmidt to tell him about the episode.

"Any idea who it was, Grace?" he asked.

"Had to be the Order. The question is, how do they know where I am?"

"Leave it with me and I'll look into it," the billionaire assured her.

"You had a mole in your midst once before, Johann," she pointed out.

"Not anymore," he said firmly. "Leave it with me."

The hotel management gave Grace a new room but by the time she was ready for sleep, it was time to rise.

Showering as best she could before pulling on jeans and a shirt with a dark blue coat, Grace went downstairs and ate a breakfast of cereal, juice, and toast. Once that was demolished, she went for coffee. Strong and black.

A black cab took her to the Hall of Records where she met with the curator, Calum Hendricks. He was a tall, hawkish faced gentleman with a Scottish accent, maybe late forties. He took Grace downstairs to a large room and pulled out three boxes. Large, heavy, full of documents. "This is what you want, girl. Somewhere in there is the name you're looking for."

"Have you lot not heard of digitization?" Grace asked.

"Is that something like the removal of fingers and toes?" Calum asked with a grin.

"By the time I get through this lot you'll possibly have to remove all mine," Grace replied.

So, she went to work. The Admiralty had taken control of the operation to rid the Med of the pirate scourge. Names like Luis Olvardo, Black Jim Trent, and Michel Giroud. All were pirates of renown who'd sailed the Mediterranean after returning from the Indies.

All had gone to the gallows on Gibraltar, the base of operations used by the Admiralty. But after three hours of looking, Grace had nothing definitive.

Hendriks appeared with a cup of black coffee and sat it beside her. "Get that into you, girl. You look like you could use it."

"You're not wrong, thank you."

"You been out playing with the dock workers, missy?"

Grace gave him a curious look. Hendricks touched his face. She nodded. "Midnight visitor."

"Bloody hell, I hope he looks worse than you."

"Let's just say he saw the error of his ways."

"What exactly are you looking for?" Hendricks asked curiously. "I've been here more years than I care to remember. I just might know something."

"Esteban Ariel," Grace said. "He was a pirate."

"Nope, can't say I ever heard of him."

Grace looked disappointed. She thought for a moment and said, "He was possibly amongst the pirates who were cleaned out of the Med by the Admiralty. I need to know if he was and where he would have been taken."

"The answer to the second part of your question is that all the pirates were taken to Gibraltar and tried. Nearly all of those were hung, lass."

"What about the first part?" Grace asked. "Is there a list of names?"

"There might be something in the Gibraltar records."

She followed Hendricks down a row of shelves until he stopped halfway along. He took down a box and passed it to her and then took one himself. "What are these?" Grace asked.

"Trial records."

"Really? They kept things like this back then?"

"They did, lass, they did. Very strange, I know."

They removed the lids, and Hendricks left her there for another two hours while she searched. Trials and hangings were the order of the day back then. Every one of those hung was done so from the yardarm of a two-decker called *HMS Kingston.*

Pope, Morris, Lazenby, and Grierson were those who sat on the bench deciding who was guilty or not and then meting out an appropriate punishment. All four were admirals. Grace kept reading and at the end of that two hours, she suddenly stopped and stared at the name two thirds down the page. Esteban Ariel. "Found you."

It took twenty minutes to read the notes. Esteban had been captured after a ship he commanded was sunk by a

British man o' war of the island of Malta. It said he was captured along with other members of his crew. What caught Grace's eye was the mention of a tattoo. "It's them," she whispered. "The Order."

She continued and came to the part of the trial, and she read the last line. *'Executed on the 15th June on board the HMS Royal Oak.'*

"Did you find anything, lass?" Hendricks asked.

"Yes, here." She pointed at the entry. "He was captured, tried, and then hanged aboard a ship named *Royal Oak*. Except all the others were hanged aboard *Kingston*."

Hendricks frowned. "Let's see if we can find out why."

For the next ten minutes they both searched deeper through the records and found nothing. Grace leaned back in the chair and let out a sigh. "There has to be a reason he isn't in here."

"Do we have a date?"

"Yes, fifteenth of June." Grace frowned. "Wait."

She went back to the other executions. She pointed at the date. "Look. Thirteenth of April."

"That could mean he was captured later than the others," Hendricks theorized.

"No. He was captured off Malta before the others were hanged."

"So they waited."

"But why did they wait?"

Hendricks was about to speak when the sound of footsteps echoing on the hard floor reached out to them across the rows of shelves. The curator gave her a puzzled expression. Grace said, "Is there anyone else in here?"

"Not supposed to be, lass."

Grace took her P30 from behind her back. Hendricks

looked surprised. "Good Lord, girl, how on earth did you get that in here?"

"I'm what you'd call resourceful."

Hendricks grinned and produced his own weapon. A 9mm Walther PDP. "Me too. Now, how about you tell me what this is all about."

"Oh, shit," Grace said with more than a hint of surprise. "The Spanish Order."

The curator nodded. "Bloody pirates. It always is."

The first set of footsteps was joined by a second, then a third. Grace said, "This just keeps getting better."

"We'll split up," Hendricks told her. "This should be fun."

"If you say so."

They disappeared into the depths of the shelves of records and found killers waiting for them.

13

BLOOD ON THE STREETS

London, England

Grace reloaded and racked a round into the chamber of her P30. She felt blood running from the graze in her left arm and tried to block out the burning pain. "Fucking assholes," she muttered under her breath.

Up until this point, she was sure she'd killed one of the armed intruders and wounded another. Now a third was stalking her. She hadn't seen Hendricks since they had split up, but there was still gunfire coming from the far side of the records hall.

Grace eased her way between the end of two shelf stacks to emerge in another row. Suddenly at the other end a shooter appeared and opened fire with an Agram 2000 submachine gun. Bullets howled along the aisle catching boxes, chewing chunks out of them and scattering confetti-like debris through the air. Grace ducked back. "Bloody hell."

She waited for the burst to finish before leaning around the corner of the shelves and firing five rounds towards the shooter. Another appeared behind her and opened fire. This one had a handgun but sprayed rounds like it was a heavy machine gun.

In desperation, Grace dived forward and rolled across the aisle and came up on a knee. She fired twice at the new shooter and saw them buckle after a bullet took them in the thigh. She took a better aim and fired again. This time the shooter's head snapped back, and they dropped dead.

Grace rested her shoulder against the end of the shelf row and waited as a new round of automatic fire hammered into the boxes close by. Suddenly a curse reached her ears just as the firing ceased abruptly. She leaned around the corner and fired, the bullets hitting the shooter who was more intent on his jammed weapon than his own safety.

He died where he stood and Grace came out of hiding, weapon raised as she crept forward. No other shooters appeared, and the large room seemed to be quiet.

Grace checked the fallen shooters to ensure they were no longer a threat. They had tattoos. Then a voice said, "Are you all right, Lassie?"

She let out a sigh of relief. "I'm good."

Hendricks appeared, a tear in the sleeve of his suit. Grace saw it and said, "You're hurt."

He nodded at her. "Speak for yourself."

"These people, I'm suspecting they're from the Order."

"Aye, it's possibly true. But don't worry, I'll take care of everything. Just wait here."

"Wait. What?"

But Hendricks was gone.

———

True to his word, the Scotsman took care of it. By the time everything was done, the bodies were gone, and a woman had taken care of Grace's wound. When he reappeared again, Grace said, "Just who are you?"

"We're Custodians of the Records," he replied.

"What do you mean?"

"Well, Lass, like you have the Spanish Order, the Hall of Records has Custodians."

"Like some kind of secret protection force?"

"That's it. If some of the secrets we guard down here ever reached the light of day it would change the course of history."

"Can I see them?"

Hendricks just grinned.

Grace gave him a wry smile of her own. "I guess not."

"We keep them in a separate part of the building which only Custodians can access," he informed her.

Grace nodded. "Thank you for your help."

"We're not done yet, girl. We need to find out why your friend was hung away from the others."

"The man who attacked me in my hotel was British. I'm just wondering if these were too? They had tattoos."

"Intriguing," Hendricks said. "I think I might know someone who can help. A former navy man who knows everything there is to know from back when the pirates were in control of the Med."

"That sounds good."

"Come back later today, around two. I finish then. I'll take you to meet him."

"Thank you, Mister Hendricks."

"Calum."

"Grace."

He nodded. "I'll see you then."

————

Grace waited for the phone to be answered.

"Hello?"

"Hey, Molly, can you set up a conference call with Johann?"

"Sure, Grace, give me a minute."

True to her word, a minute later, Johann Schmidt came on. "Hello, Grace, how are you feeling?"

"I'm all right, Johann. I just called to update you on the situation."

"I'm listening."

"I met a man today—a most interesting man, actually. His name is Calum Hendricks."

"Yes."

"I'm meeting him later this afternoon," Grace informed him. "He is the curator at the Hall of Records."

"Why do I get the feeling you are leading up to something?" Molly asked.

"Maybe because I am. Johann, was there something you're not telling me?"

"Like?"

"That the Hall of Records has its own security service called the Custodians?"

"Oh, that," Schmidt replied. "Didn't I mention it?"

"Ah, no, you didn't."

"Unforgivable."

"Just as well he was there. There was more trouble."

"Are you alright?" Schmidt asked, his tone changing.

Grace said, "I'm fine. But I found out something I think is interesting. Ortega, if it was Ortega, was hung later than the others on a different ship. Molly, I'll send you what I know."

"Send away," Molly replied.

"Is there any indication why they would do that?"

"No, not at the moment. Calum is going to take me to

meet with a man he knows. Hopefully he will be able to shed some light on the situation."

"I was hoping you would find something we could take to Interpol, but what we have is nothing. Have you heard from Brooke or Mark?"

"No."

"Another troubling situation. Anyway, let me know what happens."

"Yes, sir."

Molly said, "I'll see what I can dig up on this end."

———

Hendricks took Grace to a large building overlooking the Thames near Tower Bridge. The man they were looking for had an office on the top floor. Howard Grayson was a former admiral with the Royal Navy. Now he ran a private firm that supplied security teams for shipping lines to defend against pirates across the globe.

The man sat behind a large wooden desk made from timbers rescued from an old man o' war, *HMS Doubtful*. Grayson, in his fifties, was bald, with a weathered face, and his hands were large and tough. He looked up from his desk when Hendricks and Grace were shown in. Standing, he buttoned his suit coat and held out his hand. "Calum, good to see you."

"Howard," Hendricks replied. He indicated Grace. "I'd like you to meet Grace. She has somewhat of a dilemma you might be able to help her out with."

Grayson took her hand. Its size engulfed hers. "Pleased to meet you."

"You too, sir."

"Now, what is it I can help you with?"

"What do you know about the Spanish Order?"

Grayson raised his eyebrows. "Hmm, that old stinky kipper."

"You know them?"

He nodded. "Oh, yes, I know of them. We've run across them a time or two."

Grace frowned. "I don't get it. How is it that you all know about the Order but the rest of the world doesn't."

"To the rest of the world, pirates are just pirates," Grayson explained. "But we know better. Now, what is it that they're up to?"

"We believe that they're making a dirty bomb, but we don't know the target."

Grayson glanced at Hendricks then back at Grace. "What makes you believe this?"

"They stole spent fuel rods off a ship called the *Venetian Sea*."

"Did they now? Have you told the authorities about it?"

"Nothing gets done without proof."

"Very true." The man placed a hand under his chin as though thinking.

"I came here to the Hall of Records with a name. Esteban Ariel. Full name, Esteban Ariel Ortega."

Grayson's eyebrows raised again. "A name I've not heard for a long time. Start at the beginning, lass, and leave nothing out."

So, Grace regaled him with the whole story and when she was finished, Grayson said, "It's amazing what such a small thread can lead to. Esteban Ariel, as you know him, was hanged in Portsmouth. That's where the *Royal Oak* was at that time."

Grace nodded slowly. "Do you think that could be their target?"

"Revenge? It's quite possible."

"How would they get it into the country?"

"There is an open secret that should you need to get something into the country, there is only one man who can do it without any problems."

"Who?" Grace asked.

Grayson grabbed a pen and paper and scribbled a name down. He handed it over and said, "This is the man you will need to see."

"Thank you, Mister Grayson, we should be going now."

"Good luck," Grayson said.

They left the building and stood beside Hendricks's Land Rover. Grace said, "Do you know this man?"

He looked at the name. "Unfortunately, yes. He is a nasty piece of work."

"Where can I find him?"

"I will show you."

Then just as she was about to climb into the vehicle, a bullet reached out and touched her.

———

Hendricks ducked down behind the Land Rover as another bullet cracked overhead. He drew his side arm and tried to see where the rounds had come from. Another bullet punched into the vehicle with a crash, but the loud crack of the rifle firing couldn't be heard. It was a suppressed weapon.

The two security guards outside the door of the main entrance could tell something was wrong and when they saw Grace down, one put out a call over his radio. The other guard came out into the open and as the Scotsman called a warning the guard was hit by a bullet in his chest.

"Bloody Christ," Hendricks growled.

Using the engine block as cover, he looked over the

front of the Land Rover. Another bullet spanged off the hood. Hendricks fired in the general direction of the shooter who looked to be on top of a building close by. But then the firing stopped.

Just like that.

The Scotsman slid around the front of the Land Rover and found Grace lying in a pool of blood, not moving. He felt for a pulse. It was there, but only just. Before he knew what was happening, Grayson was beside him. "Is she alive, Calum?"

"Yes, just."

"Get her up, I have somewhere to take her."

"We should inform her people."

"No, if the Order find out she's still alive, they'll keep coming. We don't know who to trust, Calum."

14

SHARK FOOD

Mirabella Bay, The Monastery

The iron door screeched open, and Carmen filled the doorway. Mark looked up at her and smiled. "Ah, it's the wicked witch of the Med. How's daddy dear this morning?"

She returned his smile with a mirthless one of her own. Today she had on an emerald-green pants suit which matched her eyes. "My father has finally decided what to do with you. If it was up to me, I would have just shot and buried you. But he is still tied to the old ways."

Mark shrugged. "May I say goodbye to the old bastard?"

"He isn't here. He's been called away on other business."

"How sad. Tell him I'll miss him."

"If you two are done playing grab ass, how about we get down to it?" Brooke growled. "I'm done fucking around."

Carmen smiled again. This time it was a genuine

smile. She said to Brooke, "I like you. You are like me. No bullshit. What you see is what you get."

"I'm nothing like you."

"More than you know." Carmen stepped aside. "Bring them."

Two armed men entered the cell and guided Mark and Brooke out through the doorway. They were escorted along a hallway to the head of some stairs which went down, not up as expected.

Footsteps echoed throughout the stairwell. Mark quipped, "Taking us down into the bowels of the earth where their torture chambers are."

"Shut up," Brooke snapped at him.

When they reached the bottom, they were surprised by what lay before them. They emerged into a large cavern, well lit, with two docks, and men working everywhere. Brooke looked around at the underground port which reminded her of the U-boat pens from World War Two. This, however, was on a much grander scale.

They were escorted along the first dock and put onto a half cabin cruiser. Two more men joined them, and one went to the console and started the inboard motor. Mark and Brooke were seated on a cushioned bench seat at the stern of the boat where they were watched over by one of the armed men. Mark said, "This can't be good."

Another men cast off the boat then jumped on. The boat pulled away from the dock with leisurely ease. It drifted for a moment and then the boat started underway as the throttle control was eased forward.

Suddenly a loud warning alarm sounded, and an orange light flashed. Then ahead of them the cliff face slowly opened almost torturously slowly, reminding Brooke of a Bond movie. "This is cool," Mark said. "I feel like James Bond."

"Then I hope Q gave you some magic tricks to get us out of this," Brooke said out of the side of her mouth.

"I was kind of hoping that maybe you had something." His face fell, now wondering how their lives were going to end.

Once the large doors were wide enough, the cabin cruiser passed through them and out into the bay before the throttle control was pushed most of the way forward. Then the bow came up and the boat set course for deeper water.

––––––––

Wearing a bikini which showed off her lithe body, Anika sat on the side of a boat. The small team she had with her were men dressed in swim trunks as they posed as recreational swimmers and divers. They had been using it as cover for the past two days watching the monastery from afar, in between swimming and diving on the reef below.

"Anika, something is happening," one of her team said.

"What is it, Karl?" she asked without turning, still staring down into the clear water watching the fish swim by.

"The cliff is opening."

Anika turned and stared into the distance. They were three miles out but still able to see, with the use of binoculars, what was happening. She grabbed a set from the console of the boat and put them up to her eyes. Karl was right; the cliff was opening below the overhang. After a few moments a boat appeared and started heading out to sea.

The boat picked up speed, and she could make out the bow wave as it punched through the almost calm water.

Anika could see men and a woman wearing green. She had red hair. "Where are you off to?"

The binoculars drifted to the boat's stern, and she saw Mark and Brooke seated there. "Well now, that can't be good."

Anika turned to Karl and said, "Get the anchor up and get ready to follow them. Just stay below the horizon."

"Yes, ma'am."

Minutes later the anchor was up, and the boat was moving.

————

The half cabin cruiser traveled for an hour before pulling up over what the depth sounder said was a jagged reef. The helmsman eased the throttle back and the bow came down. Once in neutral, the boat bobbed around with the motion of the ocean swell. Carmen motioned to one of her men who came to his feet.

"I guess this is it," Mark said.

Brooke shrugged.

Carmen came across to them and said, "This is as far as you go."

Mark shook his head. "I knew it. Pirates still make you walk the plank."

The man who Carmen had motioned to, took something out of a cooler and removed the lid. The smell came almost immediately. "If that's my last meal," Brooke said, "I'm not hungry."

Carmen gave a grin. "I don't blame you. If you knew what went in there. But no, it is not for you."

The man grabbed a ladle and began dropping it over the side so that it drifted with the current. Soon there was a large slick floating away from the boat attracting at first the smaller fish. Then the bigger ones.

Mark leaned closer to Brooke. "Are they doing what I think they are?"

"Uh, huh. It would seem so."

"What type of sharks live in the Med?"

"Small ones."

"How small?"

"Fifteen, sixteen feet."

"What? Do they breed fucking whales around here?"

"No, Just tigers, hammerheads, and…oh, great whites."

Mark looked disappointed. "Last time I take fucking Pirate Tours."

"There," the man throwing the chum over the side said, pointing at the water.

Twenty meters from the boat a fin sliced through the water, then suddenly it was joined by another one. Mark swallowed. "They look big."

Brooke stared grimly at the fins as they cut back and forth. "I bet they're hungry too. I say you go first."

"Get up," Carmen snapped.

Mark said, "Do you always do what your father says?"

"Move," she growled.

"You said you were nothing like him," Mark tried again. "You do this, and you and he are exactly the same."

Carmen's eyes blazed and she grabbed a handgun from one of her men. "If you don't shut up, I'll shoot you in the leg and throw you over anyway."

"She reminds me of you," Mark said to Brooke. "Pretty and carries a chip on their shoulder."

Brooke glared at him. "I do not have a chip on my shoulder."

Mark grimaced and held up a hand, his thumb and forefinger almost no distance apart. "Little one."

"Screw you, asshole."

"I wasn't being nasty, or anything—"

"What the hell do you call it, you vain prick."

"Now, there is no need to get personal—"

"Stick it where the sun doesn't shine, Mark."

"Really?"

"Yes."

"Really?"

"Yes," Brooke repeated.

"I hope you're right."

"Me too."

And then they lunged at two of the guards near them and all four went over the side.

———

"Get the drone up," Anika said to Karl. "I want to see what is happening."

They were still sitting below the horizon, bobbing about in their boat. Karl went to a metal box no bigger than a tea chest and opened the lid. In doing so he revealed a quad copter drone and a control panel. Moments after taking it out, it was ready to fly.

Karl then started working the controls and the drone lifted into the sky so that it almost disappeared. Then he set it on course for the boat they were following.

Minutes later they were watching the feed live streaming from the drone. Anika stared at the feed and said, "Zoom in."

The picture grew and Anika frowned. "What are they doing?"

Karl's expression changed. "They are chumming the water. Bringing in sharks."

"Shit," Anika hissed.

"There," Karl said, touching the screen.

Anika saw it. Shark fins. "Get us in there now."

She disappeared down into the saloon as the boat picked up speed. When she emerged, she had two MP5s in her hands and tossed one to a man named Horst. "Open fire once we get in range."

The boat came up onto its plane and cut through the water, spraying the bow wave high. The boat they hunted became visible in the distance. Karl said, "They just went into the water."

Anika muttered a curse. "Hurry, damn it."

The man at the helm pushed the throttle control all the way forward.

———

When Brooke hit the water, her nose filled with the stinking chum-laden liquid and made her gag. She shook her head to be rid of it as the man she'd taken over with her fought to be free of her.

There were voices shouting from behind Brooke, but she couldn't make out what they were saying. She started to punch at the man in the water and pushed away from him. Gunshots rang out and Brooke dived down to avoid bullets peppering the surface around her.

As she went down, Brooke could see the bullets burrowing through the liquid until they stopped and started to sink. She saw Mark, doing the same, one of Carmen's men chasing him. Then she saw the shark.

Three meters of gut crunching, torpedo-like force rocketing up from the depths.

Straight at Mark.

Jaws wide.

Teeth bared.

Eyes rolled back in its head as it attacked.

Brooke screamed.

The great white struck.

The water filled with a bright, diluted red as the large beast shook its head from side to side, working its jaws. Brooke shouted and a mass of bubbles escaped from her mouth.

Mark emerged from the cloud of blood, swimming down as Brooke choked on salt water. A leg drifted from the melee of turbulent water and the dismembered body and slowly sank towards the bottom.

Another shark appeared, not as big as the white. This one looked more like a tiger. He decided that the white could have his meal; he would go after the other pirate in the water.

Brooke was now out of air and needed desperately to get to the surface. She swam upward, Mark behind her. She broke the surface, coughing, spluttering.

A shout came from the boat which was now fifty meters away. Between the boat and Brooke and Mark, the water boiled as the sharks worked on their meals.

Gunfire erupted towards them, and bullets peppered the water. Brooke and Mark took a big gulp of air and went down once more.

A large shark swam past Mark making him hesitate. Brooke tapped him on the shoulder and indicated to follow her. They needed to get away from the underwater dining table as fast as they could.

He started following her and soon they had covered fifty meters and their lungs were bursting. Surfacing again, they gulped more air. They were about to dive back down when a voice said, "Would you like a ride?"

———

The boat hammered across the water, closing the distance between themselves and the pirates. Anika turned and shouted at the helmsman, "Go faster!"

"I can't."

She brought up her weapon and looked through the sights. They were too far out but what the hell. She started to fire.

The man beside her joined in and soon the two MP5s were rattling noisily. Ahead of them Anika saw someone on the other boat point in their direction. Then the boat turned and started to speed away. Karl shouted, "Do you want me to chase them?"

"No. Get Mark and Brooke out of the water."

"Why?"

"Just do it, damn you."

Karl changed course and minutes later the boat came down and stopped. In the distance, Carmen and her people were hurrying away. Suddenly two heads bobbed above the surface of the Mediterranean and Anika said, "Would you like a ride?"

———

Ortega stared unhappily at his daughter. "You not only lost two men but there is every chance that the pair managed to escape death."

"Yes."

"Who was it?"

"I think it was Anika Meyer, Kurt Stuber's bitch."

Ortega thought for a moment. Then he said, "I don't like it. Now Stuber is interfering. I want him gone. Find him and make it so."

"What about the others?"

"Stuber is a bigger threat. Plus, he has something I want."

"The Amber Room?"

Ortega nodded. "Yes. Kill him and take it."

"Fine, but I'm still uncomfortable about Schmidt and his people."

"Put a team on them. Just watch and see what they do. Should the chance arise, they should kill them—this time."

"Yes, father."

15

A LONDON BRIDGE IS FALLING DOWN

Sicily

"At last," Schmidt said. "Where have you been?"

"Tied up with something." She gave him a rundown of what had happened.

"Thank goodness you are both all right."

"It was interesting."

"How did you get away?"

"Old friend."

"Fine. I need you to go to London," Schmidt said to Brooke over the telelink. "Grace is missing."

"Oh, no. Is there any idea what happened to her?"

"The last I knew she went to the Hall of Records. From there, she was going with a Custodian to meet someone. She was attacked in her hotel room and again at the Hall of Records. She says it was the Order. Mister Webster believes she was mixed up in yet another shootout outside a building near Tower Bridge. However, that detail can't be confirmed. You have to go to London and find out. I will have Molly send you what we know."

"Who are the Custodians?"

"They're like a security force."

"We're definitely onto something," Brooke said after thinking for a moment. "The bishop at the monastery is the leader of the Order and his daughter is an assassin."

"The treasure?"

"It's there."

"Have you seen it?"

"Bits and pieces."

"Can you get it?" Schmidt asked.

"Not yet. Besides, I think we have more pressing matters at hand."

"Yes. What about Kurt Stuber's people?"

"They're still around."

Brooke looked across the room at Anika who was quietly talking to Mark. "Are they causing you any problems?"

"Not as such."

"Keep an eye out. I don't trust anything they do. When can you be in London?"

"Late tomorrow."

"Fine. Let me know when you arrive."

The call disconnected and Brooke said, "Hey, we've got to go to London."

"What for?" Mark asked.

"Grace is missing." She turned her attention to Anika. "I don't suppose you know anything about it?"

She shook her head. "No, but I can ask."

"Don't bother."

"What about the whole nuclear dirty bomb thing?" Mark asked.

"It'll have to wait. One of our own is missing. Besides, maybe Grace found out something and that's why she *is* missing."

"Only one way to find out," Mark said.

Brooke nodded. "Yes."

———

London

They flew directly from Sicily to Heathrow and then caught a cab to the same hotel Grace had been staying at. It was late in the afternoon, and they managed to check her new room, which had been held, before going back to their own. Brooke said, "We'll go to the Hall tomorrow."

Mark nodded. There had been nothing out of place in Grace's room.

Mark sipped his beer and stared at the bottle. "Not bad."

Brooke said, "If you like that stuff. I prefer the lager."

"What do you think happened to her?"

With a shrug, Brooke said, "No idea. But someone was going after her hard. She was convinced it was the Spanish Order. Hopefully we'll find out something tomorrow at the Hall."

Mark picked up the television remote and turned on the wall mounted screen. He started flicking through the channels and then stopped. It was a story about a large, brand new aircraft carrier called the *Royal Oak*. It was a nuclear ship said to be bigger and faster than anything the Brits currently had. Mark said, "That was built in the U.S."

"How do you know?" Brooke asked.

"I read something a while back. It's currently crossing the Atlantic on its way to Portsmouth."

He changed the channel and started surfing them again, settling on another news station. This one happened to be running a story about a gunfight near Tower Bridge. "Brooke," he said getting her attention. "Where did it say Grace might have been mixed up in a firefight?"

"Near Tower Bridge."

"What was she doing there?"

"I don't know. She went there with a Custodian."

"Anything else in the intel brief?"

"Just that Ortega—or supposedly—"

Mark picked up his cell.

"Hello?" It was Molly.

"Hey, babe."

"What do you want, you big hunk of man?" she shot back at him.

"I need to know what is around the area where Grace was supposedly involved in a firefight."

"We can't confirm it."

"That's OK. Just humor me. Can you have it to me in a couple of hours?"

"I'll see what I can do."

"Wonderful. Love you."

"Aww, shucks."

"Care to tell me what's ticking over in that brain of yours?" Brooke asked.

"Just trying to nail down the reason she was there."

"Aren't we all?"

For the next two hours they waited for the information. When the cell rang, Molly was on the other end. She was put on speaker and said, "This is going to cost you, Captain America. My brilliance does not come cheap."

"I'll buy you a strawberry milkshake."

"I'm going weak at the knees already. I checked around and best guess is she was there visiting Grayson Securities."

"Who are they?" Brooke asked.

"Grayson is a former naval officer who runs a security firm. They supply operators for shipping companies as onboard security."

"That's where she went," Brooke said. "It makes sense. If anyone knows about pirates, it would be them."

"My thoughts exactly."

"Then that's where we go," Brooke said. "Thanks, Molly."

"My pleasure."

The call disconnected.

––––––

The building was large and when they went inside, they were greeted and searched by extra security who found their weapons and confiscated them. The head of the security team was a tall man with broad shoulders named Morris. He looked them over and asked, "What do you want?"

"We're here to see Mister Grayson," Brooke replied.

"Who are you?"

"Brooke Reynolds and Mark Butler. We work for the Schmidt Foundation."

His gaze lingered. "Wait here."

"Happy kind of chap," Mark said.

"Let me do the talking," Brooke warned him.

"Don't trust me?"

"Not for a minute."

Mark looked around the foyer and saw that the theme was mostly nautical. Understandably so. A few minutes later Morris returned, and said, "Follow me."

They did as ordered, and were flanked by two other security men for the duration. In the elevator, Mark said, "Bit squeezy."

Brooke glared at him.

In Grayson's office, the former navy man stood as they entered. Both security escorts moved to a corner of the room while Morris placed their weapons on the desk in front of their boss. "What can I do for you?"

Blunt, straight to the point.

"We're looking for a friend. We believe she might have come here. Woman, named Grace."

With a nod the two security men drew their weapons and pointed them straight at the visitors. Mark looked cautiously at both of them and said, "I guess we might have said the wrong thing."

Grayson looked at Morris. "Check their arms."

Morris did as commanded in a none too gentle manner. Once done he said, "They're clean."

"If you're looking for tattoos, I've got a Union Jack on my ass if you want to kiss it," Mark said.

Brooke rolled her eyes.

"Who are you?" Grayson asked.

Brooke said, "Like we told your man, I'm Brooke Reynolds, and idiot here is Mark Butler. We work for Johann Schmidt at the Schmidt Foundation. We're looking for Grace Cramer. We believe she came here with a guy from the Hall of Records. We can't confirm it, best guess."

"Can you prove who you say you are?" Grayson asked.

"Have you heard of the Global Corporation?"

The former navy man nodded. "Give them a call, ask for Mary Thurston."

Grayson reached for the phone on his desk. A few moments later he hung it up and said, "I guess you are who you say you are. Sorry about the reception, but activity has picked up around here of late."

Brooke nodded. "You could possibly blame us for that."

"What about our friend?" Mark asked.

"She was here," Grayson confirmed.

"Was she involved in the shootout?" Brooke asked.

He nodded grimly.

"Where is she?"

Grayson picked up their weapons from his desk and said, "I'll take you to her."

He led them downstairs to the parking garage where they found five SUVs lined up in a row. Mark leaned close to Brooke. "Military anal."

Morris went to the rear of the closest SUV and opened it. He started handing out vests and passed the last two to Brooke and Mark. "Bit extreme?" Mark asked.

Grayson finished slipping into his while checking his SIG P229. "Like I said, activity has picked up of late."

By the time they were ready to go, all five SUVs had men in them. Brooke and Mark were to ride with Grayson who sat in the front passenger seat of the third SUV.

The former navy man reached for his radio and said, "Let's move. Take London Bridge."

————

The man behind the binoculars lowered them and said into his comms. "We have movement from the parking garage. It has to be him."

"Is there any sign of the targets?"

"No. But we have to assume they're there."

There was a long silence.

The man with the binoculars said, "What do you want to do? It is a chance to get two birds with one stone."

"Then let's get those birds. All teams, go. Get the heli-copter up."

————

"We've picked up a tail." The voice came from Morris at the head of the fast-moving column. "Razor Five reports three vehicles, closing."

"Just three?" Grayson asked.

"Yes. What do you want to do?"

"Just monitor them. Take Tower Bridge. Let's get across."

"Yes, sir."

Mark looked out the window and at the buildings flicking by, then he saw something through a gap. He frowned. Stared. Saw it again.

Mark's eyes widened. "Skipper, we've got a helicopter to our right tracking us."

"Where?"

"There—shit, helicopter inbound. He's going to fire."

And it did.

An MH-6 Little Bird with miniguns and rocket pods. Like a raptor of the sky.

It opened fire.

Twin streaks of smoke reached out like lances.

Impact was imminent.

Then the convoy turned.

The rockets impacted the pavement throwing great chunks of concrete into the sky. The convoy started across Tower Bridge, desperately trying to get to the other side. But it all came to a sudden stop.

"Road block! Road block! Road block!"

"Everyone out," Grayson said calmly.

Chaos began to reign on Tower Bridge. People were abandoning their vehicles, and running toward the far end of the bridge. The MH-6 swooped in low, miniguns blazing. Vehicles erupted into flames, civilians died, some disintegrated. Morris once again went to the rear of his SUV, retrieving two spare M6A2 assault weapons. He threw them to Brooke and Mark along with some spare magazines. "I hope you can use them. If you can't you're about to learn. Good luck."

Mark charged his weapon and looked at Brooke. "He says it like he knows we're going to die."

Brooke nodded. "Let's prove him wrong."

She came up and opened fire to their rear where the pursuing vehicles had disgorged their passengers. The other shooters from Grayson's security firm were doing the same. Brooke saw a man go down, followed by a security specialist.

Suddenly Grayson was beside her, firing his weapon like an old soldier. "Bloody bastards," he hissed as he changed out his magazine.

"Slow down, Grayson," Brooke shouted at him. "You're wasting ammo."

"It makes me pissing feel better."

The helicopter came back around and fired a pair of rockets. One of Grayson's SUVs towards the rear of the small convoy exploded in flame, enveloping his men sheltering behind it. Cries of pain echoed, and Brooke ducked back down as the helicopter swept low, dodging around the towers.

"Fall back," Grayson snarled.

He started jogging towards the base of the closest tower. Brooke came up and fired a long burst with the M6 to cover the retreat. Mark did the same before they too started hot on the security man's heels.

The shooters from the other side increased their rate of fire and the din of battle grew even louder. Glass shattered, holes opened in vehicles, people were wounded, the unlucky ones died.

A woman cried out, stumbled, and fell near Brooke. She bent down and grabbed the woman's shirt and began dragging her into cover behind a stalled truck. Brooke checked her and saw the bloodstain on her pants. She said, "You'll be fine."

"Don't leave me."

"I'll be right back."

Brooke scurried to a Peugeot left abandoned opposite her position. She saw figures leapfrogging across the bridge in their direction. Aiming the M6, she fired with deliberate precision. Seeing a man fall, Brooke aimed at another when the MH-6 did another sweep. This time, it fired rockets and miniguns.

The latter sounded like the atmosphere was being torn apart and a long stream of incoming rounds ripped through everything it touched. But then came the rockets. The first hit a stationary vehicle, the second hit the truck Brooke had been sheltering behind along with the wounded woman.

The blast threw Brooke to the ground, her head hitting the door of the Peugeot. The blow stunned her, making her ears ring. A warm wave washed over her from the burning truck and as her vision cleared, Brooke saw the blackened figure lying next to the large pyre.

Brooke's face screwed up in anger. "Dirty rotten motherfucker."

She sprayed what was left in her magazine at the approaching shooters before dropping down to reload.

Mark appeared beside her. "You coming or hanging out here?"

She gave him a curt nod. He saw the thin trickle of blood running from her hair line. "Are you alright?"

"I will be," she replied. "Let's move."

They ran towards the tower, zigzagging between the stalled vehicles. When they reached the structure, they sheltered inside the large archway over the street. It was there they found Grayson, Morris, and what was left of his security force. Below their feet the lazy brown waters of the Thames flowed by, oblivious to what was happening above.

Mark looked across at Morris. The security boss said, "I see you're still alive."

"I'm hard to kill. Just like a cockroach."

"He's got the cockroach part right," Brooke said dryly. "What now?"

"We wait," Grayson said.

Mark was staring out through the tunnel entrance from his position of shelter when he saw the MH-6 helicopter coming back around. He said, "You might want to figure something else out, because that idea is shit."

The helicopter fired two more rockets. Both hammered into the top of the tower above them and exploded thunderously. Orange flames leaped skyward, and debris fell, crashing down. Inside and out.

"Jesus Christ," Mark growled as he dragged Brooke to him, wrapping his arms around her, covering her head.

A large solid block from the tower fell from above like a meteorite crashing to earth. It hit one of Grayson's men, killing him instantly, his head split like a melon.

Suspension cables parted and the iconic bridge built in the late 1800s, was threatening to fall into the river below.

"We need to get out of here," Mark said to Brooke, letting her go.

She nodded. "I agree. Grayson, we can't stay here."

"No shit. Clive, get them moving."

Morris pointed at two of his men. "You two, watch our rear. The rest of you, follow me."

They all left the crumbling tower and started across the debris strewn drawbridge. As they crossed it, Brooke looked up and saw one of the two upper footways was missing, and the second was damaged.

From their right came the MH-6 once more, miniguns

blazing. Mark and Brooke dived behind an Audi which had been abandoned and its roof crushed by falling steel from above. Pinned beneath it was the body of a man, eyes wide in death.

Heavy caliber rounds once more chewed up everything they touched, including Morris, Grayson's head of security. One moment he was there, the next he was just a shattered lump of meat.

"Clive!" Grayson shouted as he saw his man blown apart. "Blast. Keep moving. Get off the fucking bridge."

Mark made to get to his feet, but the strength of Brooke pulled him back down as a shooter opened fire and 5.56 rounds cut through the air where his head had been. He took a deep breath and said, "Thanks."

Brooke fired at the shooter who disappeared behind a Land Rover. "Move!"

Mark came to his feet once more and started running, followed closely by Brooke. A vehicle exploded behind them. Ahead of him, Mark saw a small girl, maybe four or five, crouched next to the body of a woman.

With a bitter curse, Mark stopped and crouched beside her. The woman was dead. Her eyes were open, her head had a misshapen look about it. A piece of debris lay nearby. The woman however didn't look like the child. "Is that your mother?"

"N—no, nanny," she stammered.

Mark nodded. "We can't stay here."

He wrapped an arm around her, picking her up, and started to jog the rest of the way across the bridge, his M6 in his opposite hand.

They reached the far tower and he put the little girl down. He grabbed a woman sheltering there and said, "Get her out of here."

The woman swallowed hard and nodded before

disappearing. He turned and saw Brooke. She said, "Where's her mother?"

"No idea. The child was with her nanny. She's dead."

The shooters opposite them pressed forward, bullets peppering all around the tunnel opening. Somewhere Brooke could hear the beat of the helicopter blades as it came around again.

Then the world seemed to explode in a fiery blaze and things went black.

———

Brooke coughed and dragged herself to her feet. A curtain of dust hung in the air and the sound of sporadic gunfire still rang out. She looked to her left and saw Mark still down, eyes closed, a thin line of blood trickling from his brow. She crouched beside him, the bruise on his forehead already forming. Brooke checked his pulse. It was strong.

Tapping his face gently at first, she began to slap him when he didn't respond. Mark's eyes snapped open. She smiled at him and said, "Good, you're awake. Get back in the fight."

Mark blinked and watched as Brooke got to her feet and started firing at the approaching shooters. He frowned and looked up and saw that the top of the tower was missing. "Jesus Christ."

Mark climbed to his knees and picked up the M6 which lay beside him. He looked at it and out of habit, changed out the magazine to have a fresh one ready to go. He looked around and saw the dead and wounded either lying down or standing to fight.

Mark's head spun and he staggered over to where Brooke was, and his shoulder rammed into the wall of the tower. He grunted and Brooke asked him, "Are you alright?"

"Been better. We need to stop that helicopter, or we're all screwed."

Brooke nodded. "Stay here. Don't get shot."

"Where are you going?"

"To kill me a helicopter."

She ran to an arched opening and passed through. On the other side was an internal staircase. She started upward just as the MH-6 made another gun run and bullets punched through already shattered windows.

Brooke threw herself down just as a hailstorm tattooed the wall near her head. She ground her teeth together and said, "Motherfucker."

The helicopter zoomed overhead, and Brooke came to her feet then started running up the stairs.

Until she reached a platform and found she could go no further. The top of the tower was gone, everything was open. She could see London as well as the river.

And the MH-6.

It was circling like a vulture. It banked over the city and started back, approaching along the Thames. Brooke dropped out the almost spent magazine from the M6 and reloaded it with a full one.

Bringing the weapon up to her shoulder, she looked through the sights. Then she waited.

The helicopter opened fire.

The air was filled with death.

Brooke waited.

The MH-6 fired its last two rockets.

They hammered into the bridge, shaking it to its core.

Brooke waited.

Then at the last minute she opened fire and prayed for a miracle.

One that was answered.

The helicopter seemed to falter and then dipped. It started to drop from the sky, its pilot dead at the controls. The MH-6 crashed in a ball of flames onto the bridge. The explosion of aviation gasoline, when it ignited, erupted upwards engulfing suspension cables and supports. They all parted and hung uselessly downward. With one look, Brooke shook her head. "Oh, shit."

She took the stairs three at a time until she was down.

"Get off the bridge! Get off the bridge!"

Mark looked at her. "What is it?"

"The cables are compromised as well as the span. We need—"

CRACK!

The whole bridge shook.

And started to fall, crumbling beneath their feet.

It was too late. Tower Bridge was coming down.

———

"Move! Move!"

Brooke ran for the rail. Mark was close behind her. The bridge started to give way and fall into the Thames. By the time they reached the rail, the drawbridge span was already in the river.

Brooke threw her weapon away and leaped over the rail. She fell for what seemed like an eternity before she hit the cold, murky water.

Mark landed behind her.

She clawed at the water, pulling herself towards the surface. Brooke's head broke clear, and she took a deep breath. Then she looked up and saw the remaining tower falling right towards her.

"You have got to be fucking kidding."

Brooke dived down just as the tower hit. She felt the

force of the displacement as it shoved her aside. Somehow the miracle was complete as it slid past her.

Her vest, however, began acting like a diving belt and she fought to discard it, eventually freeing herself from the weight.

Only then did she kick her legs and propel herself back towards the surface of the Thames. Once her head was above water she looked around and saw Mark holding Grayson afloat. Relief flooded her. "Are you alright?"

"I'll live. Help me get Grayson ashore."

"What's wrong with him?" Brooke asked as she paddled towards them.

"I think he got clipped by some debris. Did you see that damn tower come down?"

The memory was still vivid. "You could say that."

Brooke helped get Grayson to the bank, and while Mark checked him, she looked around. The shooting had stopped and Tower Bridge—the once iconic structure— was no more. She shook her head. "Holy shit."

"You can say that again."

"Johann is going to kill us."

"He needs to get in line."

Sirens could be heard in the distance echoing across the river but getting louder as they approached. Grayson coughed as he came around. He looked at Brooke and Mark and said, "Did we sink the bastard?"

Mark chuckled. "We sure did, Admiral. We sure did."

"Time for you to go, son."

"We need to stay with you."

"I'm bloody fine." He looked at Brooke. "Sixteen Lilliput Lane."

"What?"

"That's where you'll find your friend. Go there. They'll help you."

"But—"

"Go, get out of here. That's an order. I'm fine."

Brooke looked up at Mark. "Come on."

Mark and Brooke got him up top and lay Grayson down. "Take care, Admiral."

"Don't you worry, it'll take a lot more than a bloody bridge to slow me down."

They stood up, gave the former navy man one last look, and started jogging away from the devastating destruction of an English icon.

A few minutes later a shadow fell across Grayson, and he opened his eyes. "I thought I told you to—"

WHAP!

His brains were punched out the back of his head.

16

THE ENEMY OF MY ENEMY

Somewhere in Europe

Kurt Stuber picked up the apple from the display basket and smelled it before taking a bite, marring the beauty of its bright red exterior. He dug into his pocket for some coins and passed them over to the stall holder.

The stall holder thanked him and put the money in his apron pocket. Stuber continued on his way through the village market.

He was a man in his late forties, had blond hair bordering on platinum, with an average height and build. However, he was one of the wealthiest men on the planet. If not monetary, then in material.

He was a treasure collector, and collector meant thief. Stuber acquired treasures by any means possible.

His current project, and most prized possession, was the Amber Room. At that very moment, it was under construction less than five miles away from where he stood.

And when it was done it would be the most magnificent prize in his collection. But his immediate problem was the band of killers who called themselves the Spanish Order and the treasure in their possession from the *Golden Hawk*.

One other concern was Anika's involvement with Mark Butler. He couldn't have one of his own sleeping with the enemy. He would talk to her about it again.

Stuber stopped and picked up a small ornament from a table at a different stall. This one had a lot of little trinkets and collectibles scattered across it.

"You want to buy?" the man behind the table asked. "You always look, but not buy. Same one, all the time. You buy today?"

Stuber nodded. "How much?"

"For you, because it is ugly and you like so much, four Euro."

Stuber nodded. "Two."

"You drive a hard bargain. Three?"

"All right." Stuber took out the money and passed it over. "Don't spend it all at once."

The man shrugged. "It will get me a coffee."

Stuber looked at the item in his hand. Handmade, third century, maybe worth a hundred thousand Euros. The stall man had no idea what he'd had in his possession.

He put it into his pocket and kept walking. Across the cobbled street where the other stalls were, Stuber's two bodyguards tracked his every move.

He walked further on, stopping occasionally to look at something that caught his eye, and then went to a café to grab a coffee. He ordered two extras for his men and then sat at a table to drink it. He looked around. There were six café patrons. Three tables had two people each. Four men, two women, chatting.

Stuber finished his coffee and rose from the table before starting along the street once more.

Ahead of him was a black Range Rover, highly polished, and awaiting his arrival. He climbed into the passenger seat and turned to his driver. "Take me home, Ernst."

The rear doors opened, and the other bodyguards climbed in. The driver started the SUV and eased away from the sidewalk.

————

"Target on the move," Carmen said in a soft voice. She remained at the café table as she watched the SUV pull away.

Gone was the standout red hair, replaced by a glossy raven wig. She wore jeans and a white tank top and dark sunglasses. Across from her, Marco sat sipping his coffee. He placed the cup on the table and said in a low voice, "Bring the car around."

Moments later a dark blue Volvo appeared in the street and Carmen and Marco left the table and climbed into the back. Carmen said into her comms, "Sitrep, Team Two."

"We are following the target."

"Good, do not get seen. Remember, we only want to know where he is residing. The rest will happen tonight."

They drove for a few minutes and then the call came. "Target entering an estate."

"Keep driving," Carmen said. "Do not stop."

The follow SUV drove past the entry while the one Carmen was in slowed and eased to a stop a few hundred meters from the estate. She turned to her bodyguard and said, "Marco, have a look."

Marco leaned down and picked up a small case from the floor and opened it. Inside was a small Nano Drone not unlike the Black Hornet. It looked like a small heli-copter with an overall length of five inches.

Within a couple of minutes, Marco had the window of the Volvo down and the drone in the air. It sent a signal back to the small laptop Carmen now held and recorded with.

"It looks very large," Carmen said. "I can already see roving patrols. And security cameras."

Marco kept the drone flying, mapping the grounds and the building, as well as all the security guards.

"Stop there," Carmen said.

She studied the screen. "Zoom in on that object in the lawn."

The thing in question grew bigger as the camera zoomed, and appeared to be a pipe cap. Carmen frowned. "Switch mode."

Marco pressed a button and the picture changed. It revealed a large chamber below the ground approxi-mately double the size of the house. "Well now, that's interesting."

Carmen nodded. "There are a lot of people down there."

"Are you thinking what I'm thinking?" Marco asked.

"Change view."

Once more the picture changed, and they could see the outline of large crates and other objects all in rows. Except for one end of the underground chamber where there looked to be a large room. But there were at least seven people in the room, all working on something. Carmen said, "We need to get in there."

"What about the priority target?"

"We kill him first. Two teams. I will lead the team on the house. Your team will find out what we're looking at."

"I'm going to need a prisoner to question. Someone who knows how to get down in there."

Up ahead the gates to the estate opened. An SUV appeared and turned in the opposite direction. It drove slowly away and kept going. Carmen said, "There's your chance."

———

It took three toes and two fingers for the man to talk. For a moment Marco and Carmen thought he would remain silent but eventually he cracked, his screams filling the dark room.

The large underground chamber was Stuber's treasure room. Everything he had was stored there.

"He doesn't have much," Marco observed. "It's only half full."

The man shook his head. "That is the first level. There are three levels."

"Three?" asked Carmen.

"Yes. Every chamber has crates in it."

"What about the empty room where the people look like they're doing something?" she asked.

"The assembly room."

"What do you mean, assembly room?"

"Where they're assembling the Amber Room."

Carmen glanced at Marco. "Things just got really interesting."

"How are we meant to steal it if they're putting it together?" he asked her.

"Let me worry about that." She turned her attention back to the tortured man. "How do we get into the treasure chamber?"

"Through the garage. It has a twenty-ton elevator which will take a lorry."

"How else? That can't be the only way?"

"There are two other ways. A tunnel from the house and a stairwell in the garage."

Carmen nodded. "Tell my man the rest. All that he asks you will give him answers to. Understood?"

"Then you'll set me free?" A spark of hope lit the man's eyes.

She smiled at him. "Oh, without doubt."

She took Marco aside and said, "Once you have all you need, kill him. I need to talk to my father."

Carmen went out into the waning sunlight and took out her cell. She was about to dial when Cosimo appeared, a concerned expression on his face. "Princess, there has been a problem."

"How bad?"

He passed her the tablet he'd been holding. She looked at the screen. A video was playing on it. "What is this?"

"What's left of Tower Bridge in London."

Then she realized, that's exactly what it was. Amid the fires and the damage, she could make it out. "What happened, Cosimo?"

He gave her a rundown.

"A helicopter?"

"Yes."

Carmen shook her head. "They shot down our fucking helicopter. Jesus Christ. What happened to working in the fucking shadows?"

Cosimo remained silent.

"My father will fucking love this."

"Maybe he won't find out."

"The man knows everything." She shook her head again. "Thank you, Cosimo."

Carmen made the call. The first words out of her father's mouth were, "A helicopter?"

She rolled her eyes as a bird flew across the darkening sky. "Yes, father."

"You need to clean it up, Carmen."

"How? Do tell me. It's just a massive fuckup which can't be undone."

"Language, daughter—"

"Fuck the language. You need to forget whatever it is you have planned and we—I mean all of us—need to go back into the darkness until this all blows over."

"We have come too far for that, Carmen." His voice was cold, harsh.

"Damn it, father—"

"I will not have you question me, Carmen. And I will not discuss it with you. Now, have you found our friend Stuber?"

"Yes."

She went on to tell him all that she knew, all the while, her anger was roiling beneath the surface. Ortega listened and when she was finished, he said, "Make the treasure secure and then we can organize to have it moved. No one is to be left alive, Carmen. No one."

"I understand."

"Now, I have to be in Romania."

"Why?"

"I do not answer to you." His answer was curt.

She bit back another harsh retort. Her father would ruin everything for his endgame, whatever it was to be. "Can it not at least wait? This thing that you are doing?"

"No, it cannot. Now, don't speak of it again."

"Yes, father."

The call disconnected. She was now more certain than ever. She was going to have to kill her father just as he had killed his own. Yes, that was right. She knew that he had murdered her grandfather. Cut his throat as he lay in his bed and then used Olvado, a much younger Olvado, to get rid of the body.

Carmen had seen him doing it, hence her hatred for her father's man.

He would have to die too. She would see to it personally.

———

Both teams were dressed in black, wearing combat gear, and carrying MP5SDs. Carmen led the assault team on the house while Marco took the treasure chamber. Using hand signals, Carmen directed her team as they breached the perimeter. Snipers were deployed as well as an overwatch.

As the two teams crossed the ground, shooters from Stuber's security force appeared. Weapons opened fire but only short bursts because those who weren't taken down by the snipers were killed by the pirate teams.

Carmen shot one security man who appeared around the corner of the main house. The power had been disabled, and she was wearing night vision like the rest of her team. The man appeared in the green haze, and she stroked the trigger twice and he dropped like a stone.

They moved swiftly towards the house and started to secure it. Her team fractured into three smaller teams as they cleared rooms. Stuber was found downstairs in his den, sitting behind his desk waiting as though resigned to his fate.

Torch light shone on his face as Carmen stood in front of him, flanked by two of her men. She was about to speak when Marco's voice said, "We have secured the treasure room. Shall we bring the trucks in?"

"Yes. Just the room."

"Princess—"

"Do it."

"Yes, mistress."

Carmen looked at Stuber who said, "Did your father send you?"

"Yes."

"I always knew this time would come."

"Then why didn't you try to stop it before it happened?" Carmen asked.

"Because of your mother. I knew that if I went after your father, that you would be mixed up in it somehow. And I couldn't have that."

"I guess you changed your mind."

Stuber nodded. "Anika is very headstrong."

"Then why didn't you call her off?"

"Because deep down I know your father is up to something terrible and if it happens, that would be worse. Do you know what it is?"

"No."

"She had the most beautiful red hair. You look just like her, you know?"

Carmen shot him.

————

Carmen met Marco outside and he showed her down to the treasure chamber. It was huge, but overall, there wasn't much to see. The power had been switched back on and she could see rows and rows of shelves and crates. "Show me," she said.

He took her to where she wanted to go. It was a wonderous sight, even though the room was only partially built. Her eyes lit up and she couldn't help but gasp at it. Marco said, "Where do you want it sent?"

"What do you mean?"

"I've known you for too long, Princess. The monastery is compromised. Where do you want it sent?"

"Belize."

"The Myans?"

"Yes."

"What will you tell your father?"

"We will tell him it wasn't here. Get the room to the John James. The sooner it is at sea, the better."

Marco looked troubled.

"What is it?" Carmen asked.

"The truck drivers. Your people are loyal to a fault but—"

Carmen nodded. "Kill them."

"I understand."

17

TWO PROBLEMS ARE BETTER THAN ONE

Romania

The wind was strong at that altitude and the heavy snow made the conditions much worse. On each side of the helicopter were great gray crags of cliff faces that stood like giant walls, guiding them towards their destination.

Ortega felt the helicopter buck once more as he looked at the mountains. It was a solitary place. Cold, lifeless. Much like him.

"We will be landing shortly, sir," the pilot said.

Ortega nodded. Then as they rounded a large outcrop there it was, nestled on a clifftop, built out of the stone which surrounded it.

You chose well, my friend.

The wind buffeted the helicopter as it came in to land. It rocked and lurched, snowflakes whipping around it. Then the helicopter touched down on the landing pad and the pilot shut the engine down.

Ortega climbed out and was met by Olvado. He escorted Ortega inside the building and a large iron door slammed shut with a deep boom. "I was surprised that you came, sir."

"I wanted to make sure things were going according to plan."

Olvado nodded. "I have been seeing to it myself."

Ortega frowned. "You look tired, Olvado."

"A little too much radiation, sir."

He knew what his man meant. Ortega felt a hint of sadness. Olvado had been with him for what seemed like a lifetime. Now, because of his plan, his friend was dying. "I'm sorry, Olvado."

"We all die, sir. Come, I have a surprise for you."

Ortega followed him further into the ageing complex. It was damp and smelled musty. They walked along high-ceilinged hallways, their footsteps echoing loudly. Then from there they went down into what seemed to be the bowels of the mountain. The lower they went the colder it seemed to get.

Olvado led Ortega through a rusted iron door, and they found themselves in a large room. At its center was a tented area. As they approached it, Ortega could see a figure inside moving around. They stopped and the man inside turned around. It was the professor. He was wearing a protective suit and there looked to be a radiation monitor attached to it.

The scientist came out and removed his helmet. Ortega could see that the professor was in a shocking condition. His eyes were red, he had lesions, and looked as though he could drop dead at any time. Ortega pointed at the monitor. "Was that not working?"

"The batteries went flat. By tomorrow I will be dead."

Ortega glanced at Olvado. The big man knew there was concern in the questioning stare and he said, "He will be finished in an hour."

"Then it will be ready?"

"Yes."

"I will organize transport for it."

Olvado shook his head. "I will take it, sir."

"No, I—"

"I would consider it an honor."

"All right, my friend. You shall do it."

Ortega's satellite phone rang. He knew immediately who it would be. He answered it with one word. "Well?"

"It is done. Kurt Stuber is dead."

"Good, daughter. You have done well. The Room?"

"Not here. There are other artifacts but not the Room."

"Did you not ask him before he died?"

"He would not say," Carmen replied.

"And you could not get him to talk?" Ortega asked her.

"No."

"See what you can find out."

"Are you in Romania?"

"Yes."

"When will you be back?"

"I do not know," Ortega replied.

"Father—" Carmen stopped.

"What is it, daughter?"

"Are you planning on doing something stupid?"

"It is called getting revenge for them murdering our ancestor." His voice held a sharp edge of bitterness.

"It was hundreds of years ago," Carmen shot back at him.

Ortega remained quiet as he calmed himself. Then he said, "I need you to fetch something for me from Seoul. It needs to be in London within the week."

"No, father."

There was a long pause before Ortega said, "I beg your pardon. I do not think I heard you right, daughter."

"I said no."

"Carmen—"

"I will not help you in this madness."

The call disconnected. Ortega looked at Olvado and said, "She refused. There is another way. I will come with you, my friend. This is something we should do together."

London

"You look terrible," Brooke said to Grace.

"Speak for yourself," Grace replied with a pained smile.

"A bridge coming down on top of you will do that," Mark informed her.

"Things are getting serious."

Brooke looked across the small room at the man standing against the wall. "I believe we have you to thank for her life?"

The man nodded. "Calum Hendricks."

"You are part of security at the Hall?" Brooke asked.

"Something like that."

"Pleased to meet you."

He smiled. "Your friend there is very good in a combat situation."

"Had some experience?" Mark asked.

"Former SAS back in the day."

Mark nodded.

"Wait," Grace said. "What do you mean about a bridge coming down on you?"

"Tower Bridge," Brooke replied. "You'll catch up. But the reason we're here is that Johann was worried about you."

Grace nodded. "The Order."

"They tried to feed us to the sharks," Mark told her.

"Really?"

Brooke nodded. "Yeah, if it hadn't been for Mark's new girlfriend, we'd be dead."

"Anika Meyer?"

Mark stared at Brooke and then rolled his eyes. "Have you found out anything?"

"We went and saw a former admiral named Grayson."

Brooke nodded. "We met him. He was with us when the thing on the bridge went down."

"He's dead," Hendricks said.

Mark shook his head. "No, he was alive—"

Hendricks's face grew hard. "No, he's dead."

"Shit."

"What did he tell you?" Brooke asked.

"That Ortega was hung here in London aboard the *HMS Royal Oak* under the name Ariel Esteban."

Mark looked at Brooke. Grace caught the stare and said, "What is it?"

"There is a nuclear-powered aircraft carrier in Portsmouth about to be officially named the *Royal Oak*," Mark said.

"You think that it could be the target?"

"It would be a good bet," Brooke said.

"It would be disastrous."

Hendricks said, "I have some contacts still in the Regiment. I will reach out and give them a heads up."

"It would be better if it were stopped before it got here."

Brooke nodded. "The problem being, we don't know where it is. Or how it's coming into the country."

"I swear, treasure hunting is much better," Mark stated. "Let's just go back to that."

With a roll of her eyes, Brooke said, "Good one. If we start shouting there's a bomb on the way here, what do you think will happen? I'll tell you: Ortega will use it somewhere else. Not to mention the panic it could cause."

"So, we're it?"

"Us and your girlfriend."

"She's not my girlfriend."

"I guess we'll find out."

———

Somewhere in Europe

Anika grabbed her handgun and took it out as soon as the Range Rover pulled up. She said to Karl, "Something is definitely wrong."

The pair climbed from the SUV, and she went inside. Once in the foyer, she turned to Karl. "Check the chamber."

He disappeared back outside while Anika continued.

She found Stuber at his desk where Carmen had shot him. With a sigh she shook her head. Anika didn't have to check her boss to know that he was dead.

Her cell buzzed. She took the call. It was Karl. "Everyone is dead, and the room is gone."

Anika's jaw set firm. "What about the rest?"

"It's all here."

"Kurt is dead. They killed him. Meet me back in the foyer."

"On my way."

The call disconnected but then almost immediately her cell rang again. "What?"

"Hello, Anika."

"Carmen?"

"That's right. I see you're at home. Sorry about Kurt. Orders you see."

"Where the fuck are you, bitch?"

"I'm going on a little holiday to Belize. But before I go, I thought you might like to know where a little something is."

"I will find you."

"Then you will have a choice to make," Carmen said. "Come to Belize or go to Romania."

"What is in Romania?" Anika asked.

"The bomb."

"I will get both."

"I thought you might try. I don't care about the bomb. In fact, I would rather you stopped it. However, the other I am not so keen on."

Figures appeared in the doorway and Anika threw herself sideways as gunfire shattered the room. Automatic weapons sprayed everything with deadly rounds. Anika crawled across the floor and took shelter behind an ornate sofa.

Her Glock P9 appeared in her hand, and she opened fire over the hand-carved wooden edge of the sofa. Holes appeared in the antique lounge and stuffing flew free of its velvet prison.

"Motherfucker," Anika hissed. She fired again and saw a figure fall. "Take that."

However, his friend kept firing until he had to reload, his magazine empty. Anika looked up and saw the doorway empty, guessing that the shooter was sheltering around the corner as he reloaded.

She fired four times. Twice each side. A cry of pain, the sound of a thump on the floor. Anika came to her feet, the P9 raised. She walked towards the doorway without lowering the weapon and found the second shooter dying in the hallway. Anika pointed her gun at him and shot him in the head.

Reaching for her cell, she dialed a number and the call was answered.

———

London

Brooke answered the incoming call. "Yes?"

"Kurt is dead." The words were hollow, cold.

"Anika?"

"Yes. It was that bitch, Carmen. I'm going after her."

"What about the bomb?" Brooke asked, still in shock at the news.

"You will have to take care of it. It's in Romania. I don't know where?"

"Where are you going?" Brooke asked.

"Belize. She has the room."

"Oh, shit."

"I'll text you an address. You'll find the artifacts that Kurt collected there."

"OK."

The call ended.

Brooke looked at Mark. "Kurt Stuber is dead. Carmen killed him."

"Holy shit."

"Yes, exactly. She has the room. I need to call Johann." The phone at the other end rang and Schmidt answered.

"Hello, Brooke."

"I have news."

She went into the details of what she knew and waited for her boss to respond. "Romania has a lot of places you can hide a nuclear weapon. I'll put Webster and Molly onto it."

"Thank you, Johann."

"I can't say I'm sorry about Kurt Stuber though. But I do find it odd that Anika chose to give us the location of his artifacts."

Brooke looked at Mark. "I don't understand it either. But she's going after Carmen."

"With some luck, maybe she'll tidy that problem up for us."

"Then she'll have the room," Brooke pointed out.

"Something tells me better her than Carmen Ortega. I'll get Molly to call you when we have something. Meantime, get yourself to Romania. And do not get yourself killed."

Once Johann was gone, Brooke said, "I have one more call to make."

Another number, another voice. "Hello?"

"I need a favor."

"Which means you're going to try and get me killed."

"Good possibility."

"It sounds like fun. Where are you?"

"London. I'll come to you."

18

THE EAGLE'S NEST

Hamburg, Germany

To Mark, it appeared as though the big man had gotten bigger, if that was even possible. Felix Hahn was the commander of a German Spezialeinsatzkommando squad and a friend of Brooke's. He'd grown a beard since they'd last met, and with the shades he looked like many of the special forces soldiers he'd seen in Afghanistan.

Hahn wrapped his arms around Brooke and kissed her cheek. "It is good to see you, my friend."

Brooke kissed the big man back. "And you, Felix. I hate to do this to you, but I'm afraid this is way above us and we need help."

Felix looked at Mark and extended his hand. "You, I will not kiss."

"I'm glad," Mark said, losing his hand in the big man's.

"Tell me what I can do for you."

"There is possibly a nuclear weapon—a dirty bomb—in play," Brooke explained. "At this moment we believe it is somewhere in Romania. We're waiting on a possible location."

Felix frowned. "Who knows about this…this bomb?"

"Not many. We think that if word gets out, there will be a panic and the man responsible will detonate it on a target of opportunity rather than the one intended."

"That and the fact we have no actual proof that it actually exists," Mark told him. "Nothing physical, anyway. Just the fact that the material was taken off a ship in the Med by pirates."

"Pirates in the Med?" Felix asked, raising his eyebrows.

"The Spanish Order," Mark supplied.

Felix glanced at Brooke as though he thought Mark was loco. "Is he serious?"

"Shot our plane down with a missile serious."

The big special operator was about to dismiss it out of hand but something in Brooke's expression stopped him. "Really?"

Mark said, "They fed us to the sharks."

"They obviously did not succeed, my friend."

"Thanks to Anika Meyer."

Felix frowned. "What do they have to do with this?"

"She is on our side," Brooke replied. "A tenuous ally of sorts."

"How? I bet her boss likes that idea."

"He's dead."

"Even better. Surprising, but better."

"Will you help us or not, Felix?" Brooke asked, making it sound more like an ultimatum.

The big man smiled. "It sounds like fun."

———

Berlin, Germany

Molly looked at the sour expression on Webster's face and knew he was in a mood. She reached into her pocket and pulled out a chocolate bar and handed it to the computer tech. His eyes narrowed and he said, "I have nothing."

Molly sighed and ran her hand through her colored hair. "Me neither, love. I'm beginning to think the new holocaust is beginning to overtake us."

"What's wrong?" Werner Krause called over to them from his desk.

Molly turned to him and said, "Werner, you're a smart man."

"Is there a big shit sandwich of sarcasm coming my way?" he asked skeptically.

"Where would one hide a nuclear device in Romania?"

"Conventional or unconventional?"

"Possibly being built with waste or spent fuel rods."

"Are you still working on that?" Werner asked.

"Yes."

He looked at Webster who was chomping on his chocolate bar. "There are a few places. However, my guess would be up in the mountains at one of the old Cold War bases."

Molly looked at Webster. "Why didn't you think of that?"

The computer wiz shrugged and kept eating.

"Thanks, Werner. Webster, see what you can find. If it's there, you'll find it. I hope."

For the next two hours they sifted through the gray pictures from different satellites that had passed over the country in question in the past week.

There were four possible sites. All were in the mountains. All were isolated. One showed signs of life. "That has to be it," Webster said. "There are heat signatures all around it."

Molly looked at the picture. "What is that place?"

"Back when the Russians were using it, the place was called Oryol, or Eagle. It was a nuclear weapons platform that housed long range ballistic missiles."

"It looks like someone is using it," said Molly.

"A wild stab in the dark says it is our friendly neighborhood pirate."

"Can we get a better look?"

Webster shrugged. "I can try. It looks like it's blowing up a snowstorm something fierce."

The picture changed and zoomed in. They both stared at the screen as an object came into focus. Molly asked, "Is that a…"

"Yes, a helicopter."

"It has to be what we're looking for."

"I guess we'll find out."

"I'll call Brooke."

———

Romania

The helicopter bucked as it was buffeted by the winds bouncing off either side of the mountains. Brooke looked out through the window and saw the second helicopter flying off to their left. Inside it was the second section of Felix's team. There were ten operators in all plus Brooke and Mark. Everyone was wearing combat gear and white snow suits to keep out the cold. They were all armed with Heckler and Koch G95s.

Brooke glanced over at Mark who was looking out the window at the bleak landscape as it whipped past. He sensed her gaze and turned his head. He nodded and she nodded back. She glanced at Felix who was putting a piece of chewing gum into his mouth. He grinned and offered her a piece.

Brooke took a stick of gum and removed the wrapper, tossing it aside onto the floor of the helicopter. She put it into her mouth and immediately tasted the sharp flush of flavor.

The helicopter bucked again but the operators seemed not to notice. A flash of gray-white skidded past the machine, a sign of low clouds. A voice sounded inside Brooke's ear. *"Five minutes to target."*

Out of habit from her previous life, Brooke checked her weapon again. Then she noticed that she wasn't the only one doing it. Every operator inside the helicopter was going through the same motions.

Felix stared at Brooke and pressed the transmit button on his comms. "You two come with me when we touch down. We don't know what to expect so I want you where I can see you."

Brooke nodded. Felix turned his attention to Mark. "You know which end to use?"

Mark smiled. "The one that goes bang."

"Three minutes."

Brooke looked out the window beside her and saw a tall cliff rising into a tall razorback ridge. Something flashed and then she saw the white con trail snaking through the air. "Missile left side!"

That was when the fun really began.

The helicopters parted violently allowing the missile to fly between them. Both also fired countermeasures which lit the gray sky. The passengers hung on as inertia tried to throw them about the aircraft.

Curses filled the cabin as musclebound men, and a

woman held on for dear life, praying that they wouldn't end up as a scorch mark on a gray cliff face.

In the cockpit the pilot and copilot fought to stay in control. The pilot jinked left and right then back again just as an orange flash filled the drab daylight. The copilot said, "Missile down."

"Keep an eye out for any more."

"Looks—missile right side. Target lock."

"Countermeasures," the pilot demanded as he focused on the horizon ahead of him.

"Break left! Break left! Countermeasures away."

The helicopter lurched violently once more, and the missile slid past as it lost altitude. The missile avoided the countermeasures but locked onto the heat signature from the second helicopter.

Another explosion and the second missile threat was gone. The pilot said to his second seater, "I can see the landing pad ahead."

"Copy."

"One minute."

The passengers gathered themselves and readied for insertion. The helicopter flew directly at the cliff in front of it before climbing sharply and then being thrust savagely down onto the landing pad.

Felix was the first one out, even as the second helicopter's downdraft was buffeting the big man violently. He dropped to a knee and pointed his G95 towards the doors which led into the mountain. One of them burst open and the big operator opened fire, dropping his armed target in the doorway.

Another operator crouched beside Felix just as two more shooters appeared. They opened fire and rounds cracked through the air, a couple hitting the helicopter.

Felix and the man beside him opened fire and both

shooters fell. When he glanced at the man beside him, he saw that it was Mark.

Brooke came out of the helicopter and fell in behind Felix and his men. They rushed towards the doors, stepping over the fallen bodies as they went inside what looked like to be a big hangar.

Brooke's eyes fell on the large transport helicopter sitting in the middle of the hangar. Next to it were two more shooters. The German commandos opened fire before the shooters could react, killing them where they stood.

Felix barked orders and his second team disappeared. He turned to one of his men and said something else. The man nodded and started towards a doorway at the east side of the hangar. The big German turned to Brooke and said, "It is time for the work to begin."

———

Brooke took cover and reloaded her G95. Bullets howled off the iron crate where she was crouched, and smashed into the solid concrete wall behind her. She looked across the narrow gap to where Mark was sheltering. Beside him was one of Felix's men, firing over the top of the crate he was behind.

"This is fun," Mark called out.

Brooke rolled her eyes and leaned around her cover to open fire. She let off two short bursts and then managed to hit a shooter with another. She then saw an arm wave in the air, except it wasn't waving; it was throwing a round object in their direction.

"Grenade!"

They all hunkered down just before the grenade detonated. The explosion roared loudly, sending heat from the blast washing over them. Deadly slivers sliced through the air.

Brooke muttered a curse before she started firing again. "Son of a bitch."

Another commando flanked the position and got a clear shot at the shooter. The firing stopped immediately, and the group came to their feet and continued to secure the facility.

One room at a time, working down level by level.

Brooke reloaded once more and looked down at the shooter at her feet. Something about the face caught her attention. She leaned down to examine him and then drew back. She'd seen it before. She said into her comms. "Felix, we've got a problem."

"Be right there."

Mark could see the concern on Brooke's face and went to her side. He looked down and said, "Is that?"

"I think so."

Felix appeared. He too had the same opinion. "Radiation poisoning."

"Yes," Brooke replied.

Felix pressed his transmit button and said, "Everyone hold position."

After he received acknowledgements from his men he reached into his pocket and took out a small Geiger counter. "It is high but not enough to cause this. He would have had to be exposed to something very strong."

"Right next to it," Mark said. "In the same room."

"Yes. We will keep going."

————

Felix blocked Mark from entering through the doorway in front of them. "This room. This is where it was."

He showed her the counter. It registered 350 millisieverts. Almost as much as what was registered at the Fukushima plant back when the tidal wave and earthquake occurred.

"We need to leave," Brooke said.

"Right away. The room is empty. But when they were making it, I would say that the exposure count would have been between six- and ten thousand. Just being here this long is not good. Whoever did this, wasn't concerned with safety."

Brooke nodded. "We need a prisoner."

"We're getting out of here. Everyone, evacuate to the top level. Now."

The commandos withdrew to the top level and to Brooke's surprise, the second team brought with them a friend. A wounded man who'd been shot in the arm. Brooke said, "I need to talk to him."

Felix nodded. "I'll come with you."

Mark followed them over.

Brooke stood in front of the man who had a defiant expression on his face. "Who are you?"

He spat on the floor.

Brooke took her handgun from its holster and slammed it against the man's wound. Mark winced. The man cried out in pain and staggered. Felix held him upright and again, Brooke said, "Who are you?"

Again nothing. She raised her gun and a burst of Italian exploded from the man's mouth. Brooke changed from English. "What is your name?"

"Pietro."

"Where is the bomb?"

He said nothing.

This time, Brooke didn't use the handgun. Instead, her left fist exploded forward and found the soft fabric over the bloody wound. Another cry erupted from the man before her, and he buckled at the knees. Mark winced and shook his head. "You are in the wrong game."

"Wait until I start shooting him in the legs."

Pietro understood what she said because his eyes widened. Brooke nodded. "So, you understand English. Then listen closely, asshole. I'm not going to hit you anymore. From now on, it's bullets all the way. Do you understand?"

Nothing.

"I don't have time to fuck around." The barrel of the gun went to the man's leg. "The bomb?"

"I do not know. They took it two days ago."

"Where?"

"I don't know."

"Who took it?"

"Senor Ortega and Olvado."

"Where is the professor who made it?"

"Dead. He died yesterday. We are all dead." The man pulled down the neck of his top and showed the welts which were appearing. It was then that Brooke noticed that his eyes had deep rings around them. "We were all exposed."

Brooke looked at Felix. "There goes that."

The big man nodded abruptly. "We need to track it before it leaves Europe."

Mark stepped closer. "Hey, buddy. Tough luck about that one. Being a pirate isn't all it's cracked up to be. You have family?"

He nodded.

"Italy?"

"France."

Mark nodded. "Listen, we believe that Ortega is going to detonate that bomb in the UK. If the wind blows in the right direction, there's going to be a dirty great big cloud floating across France. Your family will die just like you."

The man's eyes flickered.

"Never thought of that, did you? So, how about you help us out?"

The man opened his mouth to speak then closed it. Then Pietro said, "I heard a name. Directora."

"Director?"

"Yes."

Mark looked at Brooke. "Mean anything to you?"

Brooke glanced at Felix. "Is it him?"

The big man shrugged. "Could be."

"Who?" Mark asked.

Brooke turned back to him. "If you want something shifted in the underworld, you go to a guy called the Director. Normally, it's just things like black market goods and artifacts. Nothing heavy like weapons and drugs. It is how he stays below the radar."

"He is very good," Felix said. "He skips around a bit so he can't be pinned down."

"Then I guess we need to find him," Mark said.

"That is the big one."

19

WELCOME TO BELIZE

Belize

Anika took a small team with her to Belize. Too many would cause issues she didn't want to deal with. Once they arrived, she set about finding out where Carmen and her people were. And the one man who could help was Juan Blanco. They just had to get access to him.

Had the man been an average citizen, then no problem. But the guy was a corrupt politician who took donations from less savory characters who dealt in bribery, drugs, and death. All on a Sunday.

Yes, Juan Blanco was a bad man. But Anika was worse. He was about to find that out.

She turned to Karl. "We need him alive. Make sure the others understand."

"They understand. What they don't understand is what happens next. Where does their money come from?"

"I will pay them money."

"How, Anika? Stuber is dead."

"Let me worry about it, Karl. Just make sure everyone follows orders."

The inside of the SUV went quiet. Across the street was a large museum of Myan antiquities. That evening there was to be an unveiling of a small jade statue said to be dated around 450 BC.

Many local dignitaries were among the attendees, including Blanco.

Anika was wearing a black dress which hugged every curve of her body. A Heckler and Koch P30SK was strapped to the inside of her thigh.

Karl was dressed in a suit and was unarmed. They figured that he was more likely to be searched than Anika, her tight dress leaving few options to stash a weapon. Where could she hide a gun in that thing?

A manicured hand placed her earwig, and she said, "Comms up."

Four other voices replied.

Anika said, "Standby, we're going in."

They climbed from the SUV and walked across the rain damp street. Anika's heels created a loud clicking sound as each one hit the pavement. Her left arm was hooked through Karl's and for a fleeting moment, she found herself wondering how the others were doing with the nuclear side of things.

Concentrate.

Anika stepped up onto the sidewalk and started up the concrete stairs towards the main entrance. Karl stepped out from her side and took her hand as though he were doing the gentlemanly thing of helping her.

As she had figured, Karl was searched at the door. Anika was let in unmolested. Once in the foyer, they stopped. Looking around they were greeted by two stone statues. She guessed they had to be at least two-thousand years old, possibly more.

Anika said in a low voice, "Black and White are inside."

"Green is on the second-floor balcony."

Anika looked to her left and saw a woman adorned in a purple gown, holding a glass of champagne, looking in her direction. Standing beside her was an older man in a suit. "Who is your friend?"

"God's gift to women," she replied quietly facing away from him.

"Get rid of him."

"Can I kill him?"

"I don't care, just do it."

Anika turned back and looked at the large double doors that people were passing through in both directions. On the other side of the doors was the main display hall. That was where they would find the artifact that the night was all about, and the man they had come to find.

"Let's go," she said to Karl.

There seemed to be about a hundred people meandering around the hall, each well dressed and holding a glass of champagne. Some women wore dresses that bespoke wealth and taste. Others had been sewn into dresses that accentuated what money had bought for them. The men were a mixed bag of sweets as well. Some young, some old, some—

"Shit," Anika growled.

"What is it?" Karl asked.

"Across the other side of the room," Anika replied.

Karl looked past the pedestal displaying a Mayan jade statue and saw the man Anika had indicated, talking to a woman dressed in red. "Gunther and Polly."

"The one and only." Gunther Bach and Polly Hollister. Both were Interpol agents from the Stolen Works of Art Department. "What the hell are they doing here?"

"You should ask them?" Karl said.

Anika glared at him. "Everyone on your toes. We have Interpol in the building."

"That's not all," another voice said belonging to Red, the fourth person in the building. "I see at least three illegal art and artifact dealers."

"What do you want to do?" Karl asked.

"Continue with the mission. Red, get close to the target and stay on him."

"Yes, ma'am."

A waiter walked past carrying flutes of champagne. Anika grabbed two and passed one to Karl. "Shall we mingle?"

The pair split up and circled the room. In front of a large painting on the wall, Anika stopped and noted a work by an Italian artist from the eighteenth century. What it was doing in Belize was anyone's guess. But she suspected that if she looked into it deeper, she would find that it was stolen.

"Like what you see?" a man's voice asked in Spanish.

Anika froze before turning slowly, taking in a middle-aged man with bottle darkened black hair. Blanco stared at her, a broad smile on his face. He was flanked by two bodyguards.

"I think it is interesting," Anika replied in German.

Blanco frowned. "I'm sorry, I do not understand."

Anika switched to Spanish. "I said that I thought it interesting."

"A lot like you, I think," he replied, his eyes casually wandering over her lithe form.

His ogling eyes made her skin crawl and for a moment she found herself wanting to place a bullet into his head where he stood. Over Blanco's shoulder she could see Red not far away.

Anika said, "I am always interesting."

Blanco nodded. "I bet you are. You must join me for a drink after."

There was her in. "Why not? Your place or mine?"

His smile broadened even further. "Let's decide that later, shall we?"

"Let's."

Blanco walked away, followed by his two bodyguards.

"Why am I not surprised that you are here?"

Anika turned and stared at Gunther Bach. "Hello, Gunther."

"Are you here to steal something, Anika?" His voice was loaded with sarcasm.

A cold smile touched Anika's lips. "Not tonight, Gunther. Tonight is about information."

"I find that hard to believe," Bach snorted in disbelief. "Kurt wouldn't send his right hand somewhere without there being a valuable acquisition on the line."

"Kurt is dead."

He stared at her, trying to work out whether she was lying. Then he concluded that she was telling the truth. "Who was the lucky person?"

"Carmen Ortega."

"I can't say I am familiar with that name."

"Spanish Order."

"That is a name I am familiar with. When?"

"It doesn't matter."

"So you are here seeking revenge?"

Anika nodded.

Bach said, "You are lucky we're not here for you, or I would arrest you."

"You would try."

"We had a tip that someone was here to steal the jade idol. Seeing you here—"

A small cannister appeared and bounced across the

terrazzo floor. Anika's eyes widened as she grabbed Bach. "Down!"

They hit the hard floor just as the canister exploded. It was a stun grenade and going by the noise which filled the hall, it wasn't the only one. Then came the gas. Not tear gas, sleeping gas. As soon as it started to fill the hall people dropped to the floor.

"Gas," Anika growled at Bach.

"Is this you?" he asked savagely.

"No, you fool," she hissed and reached for her weapon.

Through the acrid cloud she saw the figures looming large. Gunshots sounded and even more people fell.

Anika could feel herself being overcome by the gas as she fought to raise the weapon in her hand. Beside her, Bach was down on his knees and faring worse than she was. Her hand fell to her side, her strength about gone. Anika slumped down and rolled onto her back.

A figure loomed over her, looking down almost curiously. Even though Anika couldn't see a face for the gasmask, she knew who it was. The red hair gave it away. Then Carmen was gone, and for Anika, the lights went out.

————

Anika's head felt as though there were a hundred little men inside it, chipping away with very big hammers, which didn't help her mood at all. Her two remaining people on the outside of the museum had her and the others out before anyone else was on site. Their mission was a bust.

"What did they take?" Anika asked.

"We think that it was only the jade statue," Karl replied.

"Just the statue?"

"Yes."

"Blanco?" Anika asked.

"Disappeared. I have one of the others trying to pinpoint him so we aren't wasting time."

"Do you think they are working together?"

"No."

"Then we need to find him."

Karl nodded. "We will have him by morning."

Anika left her people to do what they did best while she slept to get rid of the headache. The sun was up when she woke and sat on the side of the bed. Before getting up she drank a bottle of water and then put her clothes on.

The others were sleeping where they'd dropped. She walked over to Karl whose head was resting on his arms. Anika placed her hand on his shoulder. His eyes opened and he looked at his boss. "Sorry, I was just getting some shut eye."

She smiled. "It's fine. Did you find anything?"

"Yes, we found him. Getting to him might be harder now."

"Then we'll need a good plan. Or a crazy one."

Karl nodded. "I thought you might say that. Does broad daylight carjack seem crazy enough?"

Anika smiled at him again. "Oh, Karl, you make me go weak at the knees."

―――――

The plan was a simple one. Hit the convoy, shoot the bodyguards, grab Blanco, and get the hell out of it. Middle of the day, be damned.

Right at that time, the first part of the plan had worked. They'd used a stolen armored truck to ram the first vehicle in the convoy and then used a sticky charge to disable the last. Anika's team had closed in, eliminating the threats, and using a smaller charge to open the door of the SUV Blanco was in.

While Karl and one of his subordinates took care of that, Anika had taken up position at the head of the target vehicle.

A shooter had opened fire and she swung her MP5 to return fire. A long burst of fire had made him take cover. A few moments later, the shooter reappeared from behind a parked vehicle and Anika finished him with another burst.

Just heartbeats later, Karl had Blanco out of the SUV, flexi-cuffed, and with a hood over his head. "Anika, we are ready."

"Get him in the car," she snapped. "Everyone else, let's go."

Before long they had collapsed back to their vehicles and climbed aboard. Within a minute, they were away with their prisoner.

An old factory outside the city was their destination. After dragging him through the large double doors and into the cavernous building, they tied Blanco to a chair and removed the hood. He blinked his eyes several times to clear his vision in the dappled light. Looking up at Anika he demanded, "Who are you?"

"Who I am isn't important. What I want is. Do you understand?"

"What do you want?"

"Carmen Ortega."

"Who?"

"The woman who stole the jade statue from the museum," Anika said.

"I do not know any such woman."

He was lying and Anika could tell. "I advise you to tell the truth. I know you are lying to me, and I think I know why. You are working with her. Or you were. Did she betray you?"

Blanco's eyes flickered.

"She did. What were you going to do? Send the Belize Army after her?" Anika shook her head. "No, maybe not. If word got out about your little deal, your world would come crashing down. So, how were you going to do it?"

Blanco just stared at her.

"Nothing, huh? I could help you, if you help me," the woman suggested in a purr. "Get you your revenge while I get mine."

"Why would you do that?"

"She killed my boss and now I want to kill her."

Blanco looked at her suspiciously. "What is in it for me?"

Anika looked thoughtful while shrugging her shoulders. After a momentary pause as though she had actually been contemplating her reply, she said, "How about I don't kill you?"

The man nodded. "I think we can come to some arrangement."

"Then tell me where she is."

"In the jungle. There is an old mission. She has taken it over."

"What is she doing there?" Anika asked.

"I do not know. She had some trucks with crates in them. When I asked, she stared at me and said nothing. Do you know what she has?"

Anika nodded. "I could tell you, but then I would have to kill you."

———

"We can't let him go," Karl said to Anika after glancing at Blanco. "We cannot trust him."

Anika knew he was right. "Then kill him."

So, he did.

A bullet in Blanco's head.

The man protested, cried, and then died, all within seconds. Then they left him tied to the chair.

Anika turned to one of the women beside her. "I need to know where the mission is, Michelle."

"It won't take long to find."

Twenty minutes later, Michelle had satellite images in front of Anika and Karl. "This is what we have."

"It looks like they have set up a compound," Anika replied.

Michelle flicked through the pictures until she found one she wanted. "She has set up quite a team. Roving patrols, their own power source, and they're constructing outbuildings."

Anika flicked through the photos in silence. They were very detailed. Michelle had done well. "We'll draw up a plan and execute it."

"I wouldn't just go busting in there, Anika," Karl said. "She is a cunning one."

"Then we will have to be better. I aim to kill her, Karl. And I will not rest until it is done."

"Yes, ma'am."

"Where is this place, anyway?"

"Two hundred kilometers from where we stand," Michelle replied.

"Can we get a helicopter in there?"

"The closest LZ is five kilometers to the north. There is nothing closer."

"Then we will have to go the rest of the way on foot."

Karl looked at her disapprovingly. "We need more people, Anika. We will need backup in case anything goes wrong."

"We go with what we have."

"I think that this is a mistake."

Anika looked at Michelle. "You too?"

"It is not the smartest course of action, I think."

"I will take it under advisement. Get me what we need."

"What about the other thing we talked about?" Karl asked.

"I'm working on it."

He nodded. Then left.

Anika looked at the pictures and sighed. She was damned if she knew what she would do. The rainbow disappeared the moment Stuber's life ended.

————

It rained. Every one of them was wet but not one of them complained. They just trudged on through the green undergrowth towards their target. Michelle was on point, Karl brought up rear security. Between those two points, there were a further six operators, including Anika.

The helicopter had dropped them at the LZ just before the onset of the rain, turning the sky a drab gray and shrouding the jungle in low mist.

They pushed on, their gear becoming wetter with every step. Under the broad canopy of a large tree, they took a five-minute breather before continuing.

Just before dark, they found the mission and the surrounding compound. The group took up position in the jungle and watched as the last vestiges of daylight disappeared.

"We go tonight," Anika told her team.

Once more, Karl didn't like the decision. However, he would never question her choice in front of the others. Instead, he waited until they were alone. "We should take more time to observe, Anika. It feels rushed."

"Then we make sure that it isn't. Gather intel. The plan stays the same."

————

Saying with the shadows, it was just after midnight and they were making certain they weren't seen, choosing to bypass the guards. Infiltration was simple. Maybe too easy. Anika settled down near a building in the shadows and watched as another patrol walked past. Using hand signals, she ordered her people forward. They broke cover and almost immediately floodlights came on.

Every one of Anika's team froze. Beside her she heard Karl give a hiss of frustration as shooters appeared from every angle, closing the trap they had walked into.

Carmen appeared in the light. She looked smug. "Oops. Someone fucked up."

Anika just stared at her.

"Have your people drop their weapons, Anika, or I will have them all killed where they stand."

"Put them down," Anika snapped.

Weapons were dropped to the ground. Anika's jaw set firm. She stood there waiting to see what would happen next.

The expression on Carmen's face never changed. "Kill them."

The pirates opened fire, rocking Anika to the core. All around her people died, yet not one bullet found her flesh. When the firing ceased, she stood there in shock at what had just happened. Then she saw Carmen.

"What have you done?"

"Lock her away. I will deal with her at my leisure."

20

THE DIRECTOR

Bratislava, Slovakia

It was dark but the stark white of Bratislava Castle stood out under the many floodlights. The evening streets were busy but no one in the van seemed to notice. All they were concerned about was the man called the Director.

With the threat exposed, Felix had managed to rope in German Intelligence for the operation. Brooke and Mark had remained with the Special Forces Commandos but only as 'observers'.

Intel had the man they were looking for at a theater watching a play that evening. They had people outside, but no one inside. So, they had no idea what was happening. Gretel, the German Intel officer sat looking at her screen, getting more and more agitated until she finally said, "We need to get eyes in there."

Brooke said, "I'll go."

"How?" Gretel asked. "Do you even have any experience in things like this?"

Brooke nodded. "Just a little."

She let down her hair and let it fall past her shoulders. Then she removed her jacket, exposing a tight white tank top. Below that were her blue tight-fitting jeans. Mark said, "If you get through the front door, you'll be doing well."

Brooke grinned. "Hence the tank top, sunshine. If you haven't noticed, it's cold out and our friends on the door won't be too worried about the way I look, rather than what they'll be looking at."

"The woman has brains," Gretel said and gave Brooke an earwig.

Brooke climbed out of the van and started along the street. Inside the van, Gretel said, "We have an asset heading inside."

Brooke walked along the sidewalk under the watch of the large castle. It stood above like a giant sentinel. Three-hundred feet in the air, flying in almost silence, was a drone, watching her passage.

Brooke turned the corner and started across the street, approaching the stairs that led to the theater's main doors. Her boots were grinding grit on the damp surface. She stepped up onto the far sidewalk and then started up the steps. At the top she stopped and waited for those in line ahead of her to pass through the security checkpoint.

When it was her turn, the guards proved her assumption correct. Her face was ignored and when she showed them a piece of paper that had been a room receipt, they waved her through.

"I'm in."

Her cell pinged and she removed it from her pocket. Looking at the screen, Brooke saw a picture of her target. The man looked to be in his fifties with silver hair and a lined face. Looking at the once square-jawed man, Brooke thought that he might have been very handsome in his prime. Not that he wasn't now, he was just a little older.

Brooke made a judgement call and went up the wide stairs to her left. At the top she walked along the rear of the private boxes until she found an empty one.

Slipping inside and keeping to the side Brooke scanned the crowd below and the boxes she could see. "No eyes on, yet."

The lights dimmed and the show started. Brooke said, "Settle in, we're going to be here for a while."

About halfway through, they stopped for intermission. The lights came back up and people moved from their seats. It was then that Brooke spotted their target.

"I've got eyes on the target. He's going to the bathroom. Following."

"Hold position," Gretel ordered.

"I need to keep eyes on him. What if he leaves?"

"He won't leave."

"What if he does?"

"Damn it, Brooke."

Ignoring Gretel, she headed back to the top of the stairs, stopping and stepping to the side so that she didn't stand out. People filed past her as she waited for the Director to appear. It took a few more minutes but there he was.

Watching as he walked past the bathroom, Brooke knew she had been right. "He's not going to the bathroom. I'm following."

Starting down the stairs she began to shadow the target with his escort. They took a doorway that led into a long hall. Brooke hesitated before opening the door. Unarmed and following dangerous men was never a good idea.

The hallway was empty.

"I think he's headed out the back."

"Don't get too close," warned Felix.

Which was a silly thing to say.

Because nothing ever goes to plan. Or hardly ever. Like when one of the Director's bodyguards appears in front of you, blocking the way.

"Hello," said Brooke. "Just looking for the bathroom."

The man approached her. He was having none of it. He reached inside his jacket. Brooke assumed it was for a weapon and she moved.

Her right fist shot out and hit the bodyguard in the throat. He stepped back, gagging. Brooke closed the distance once more and hit him in the face. His head jerked back but this time the bigger man let out a roar of rage.

He swung a fist which caught Brooke a glancing blow on the cheek. It hurt and forced her back. Steadying herself once more, Brooke went on the attack again. She swung two punches, both were blocked, and the bodyguard stepped in close and wrapped his arms around her.

Using all his strength, he threw Brooke against the wall. She let out a cry of pain as the air rushed from her lungs. Landing on the cold hard floor, she moaned. Reaching down, the man grabbed a handful of hair. He dragged her to her feet, holding her head up.

Brooke brought up her foot and kicked him in the groin. His face screwed up in pain and he sank to his knees. A clenched fist smashed at his face, and he fell to his side.

The bodyguard's hand went under his jacket once more, this time he was successful in retrieving his Glock.

Brooke lashed out with her foot and kicked it clear of his grasp. It flew across the floor and smacked into the wall opposite. He rolled after it, his arm outstretched. Brooke brought her foot down hard on his fingers. With an audible crunch, the bones broke. The bodyguard cried out in pain.

Again, Brooke pressed home the attack. This time she kicked him in the side of the head, stunning him.

Panting, she looked around, spotting the gun. She bent down and picked it up. Then, using all her pent-up rage, she brought it down hard on his head, knocking him out cold.

She said, "The target is getting away out the back."

"We'll have someone there in a moment."

Brooke burst out through the back door and almost hurried to her death. Gunfire erupted, bullets burning through the air close to her head. She ducked down, returning fire, running to the side, looking to take cover behind a dumpster.

Bullets ricocheted off the metal bin and howled off into the night. Brooke leaned around and saw the target getting into a black SUV, his last bodyguard covering his retreat.

"The Director is climbing into a black Range Rover. Alley at the back of the theater."

"Almost there," Gretel said into her ear.

Brooke fired again and saw the shooter buckle. She came clear of her cover and opened fire again, putting the bodyguard all the way down.

Keeping the Glock raised she walked forward. The SUV started and lurched forward, only to stop when its path was blocked by the van the team was using for surveillance. Moments later the commandos appeared.

Inside the SUV, the Director lifted his hands from the steering wheel. They had their man.

———

While Felix stood in a corner, Gretel questioned him, and Mark and Brooke watched from another room.

"Hello, Edmondo," Gretel said to the man chained to

the rail across the stainless-steel table. "I always knew we'd end up here."

"Shit name," Mark said in the other room.

Brooke nodded. "Mother must have hated him."

"In Slovakia, Gretel?"

"You know what I mean."

"What do I owe the pleasure?" Edmondo asked.

"You took a job recently," Gretel said.

"I do many jobs."

"This one was for Father Juan Ortega."

"Who?"

"He is in command of the Spanish Order."

The Director cocked his head and looked at her out of the corner of his eye. "No, that doesn't ring a bell."

"Fuck this," Brooke said and left the room.

As Mark watched on, the interrogation room door opened, and Brooke appeared.

"What are you doing?" Gretel asked.

"We don't have time for this," she pointed out. "Turn the cameras off."

Gretel held out a hand and said, "I do not think—"

While she was talking, Brooke grabbed a handful of the prisoner's hair and slammed his face down onto the table.

"Jesus Christ," Gretel growled as blood spurted from Edmondo's face. "Turn off the cameras. Shit."

She whirled on Brooke. "What the fuck was that?"

"We don't have time to play footsie with this prick. He's transporting a nuclear bomb and we need to know where it is."

"I'm what?" the man known as the Director spluttered.

Brooke turned to stare at the bloody face. "Don't try to deny it, asshole."

He looked at her with a confused expression on his face. "Yes, yes, I am transporting a package through my system at the moment, but I am not transporting a nuclear weapon."

"Yes, you are."

"No—" he frowned. "No, I'm not."

"Ortega stole nuclear material from a freighter transporting it to be discarded. He has now had a scientist make it into a dirty bomb. He is using you to move said bomb to England because he has some sick fantasy of revenge in his mind."

"No, there isn't any nuclear material that I am transporting."

Brooke looked at Gretel who opened a folder she was holding and placed pictures in front of her prisoner. "Does this convince you, Edmondo?"

His face paled. "Good grief."

"Now, where is that shipment?"

"It will be transiting Germany in a lorry."

"What color?" Brooke asked.

"A blue one."

"Come on, what kind? How big?" Brooke demanded hovering over him.

"A Scania. Number BGTRB762. The tags will come back as a red Iveco but it isn't."

Brooke looked at Gretel. "I will get it out."

"They can't approach it," Edmondo said. "Ortega insisted on someone going with it. I figure I know why."

"To detonate it if it is discovered," Gretel supplied simply.

"We need to get eyes on it."

Gretel stared at Brooke. "You've done this before."

"Many times. If we can get a satellite over it or a UAV we might be able to disrupt any signal. "We'll need a mobile command post. Have you got a spare C-17 floating around?"

Gretel nodded. "Yes, but you will be an adviser only."

"I don't care what I am. Just as long as we stop this thing."

21

LIKE OLD TIMES

France

"Felix, we have eyes on the truck," Brooke said into her comms.

"We do too," the big operator replied.

His team were inside a green truck on the French Auto Route. They had only just picked up the Scania truck and were trailing it from a distance amongst the traffic headed for the French Coast.

Mark rode with them, decked out in combat gear because that was what he knew. Meanwhile, Brooke's observer status had been upgraded as soon as they were airborne. Gretel looked at the screen and said, "There are too many people on the motorway."

"There will be more if it gets into the tunnel and onto English soil. Felix, we'll try to kill the motor on the truck and jam any signals. Just be ready to go."

Felix paused. "Just to be clear, who is in command?"

Brooke glanced at Gretel. The intelligence officer said, "Brooke will be in operational command."

"Roger."

Brooke looked at Gretel. "Are you sure?"

"Just don't get us all killed."

Brooke turned to the console next to her. It was operated by a young woman in her twenties. "Find me a signal. Then track it. I'm guessing that there will be a remote trigger nearby."

"Yes, ma'am."

"Felix, can you see anything that indicates the truck is being followed?"

"Give me a moment, Brooke."

"Ma'am, I'm getting a low frequency signal close by the truck."

"How close?" Brooke asked.

"I would say within one-hundred meters."

"Felix, look for a target within a hundred meters of the target vehicle. That will be our trigger man."

"Copy."

"Mark, are you still with us?"

"Just like old times."

"Don't get yourself shot. Johann will be pissed."

"Ma'am, I've nailed the target vehicle for the signal."

Brooke and Gretel moved to look at the screen. The C-17 bucked on some turbulence and settled once more into its pattern. "Where?" asked Gretel.

The analyst touched her screen. "That one there."

Brooke nodded. "Felix, copy?"

"Copy, mother."

"You'll wish I was by the time this finishes. Lane three, two vehicles back."

"I have it," Felix replied. "An Audi sedan. Dark blue. Looks like it has three, maybe four occupants."

"One of those occupants has an electronic trigger."

"Then we need a good plan. How about a Hellfire?"

"No, out of the question."

"We need to hit the vehicle with something to incapacitate everyone long enough for us to take them out," Felix said.

"I have an idea," Mark said. "But you might not like it."

————

Ortega coughed and checked himself. He was in the back of the Audi, tired, feeling generally unwell. Radiation sickness would do that to you. He just needed to stay well enough to reach the detonation site; that was all that mattered. Beside him, Olvado's body was slumped, his eyes open, dried blood that had oozed from his body, clumps of hair fallen out. His death had come just after the border crossing into France. He'd obviously been exposed to the radiation a lot more than first thought. The same with Ortega. But this was his mission. Carmen could take care of herself now.

"Are you all right, sir?" the driver asked.

"I'll be fine. How much longer?"

"We will reach the tunnel in an hour."

"Good, good."

The driver looked in the mirror and changed lanes. Ortega caught his expression in the mirror. "What is the problem?"

"Nothing sir, just…"

"Just what?"

"I thought we were being followed. But maybe I was mistaken."

Ortega reached for the trigger in his pocket. It was transmitting; all he had to do was enter the code to detonate. "Are you sure?"

The driver looked into the rearview mirror again, watched, and then nodded. "It is fine."

Beside him the passenger checked the side mirror. "No, I see nothing."

They settled in, remaining in the same position in traffic with the truck in sight, the driver constantly checking but seeing nothing.

Then the front right tire blew.

———

"Stand by, we're about to start without interdiction," Brooke said over the open channel. "Sniper ready?"

"Yes, ma'am."

"On my mark. Three…two…one…execute."

"Sending."

"Hit, target slowing. Truck is pulling ahead."

"Standby, Felix."

"Standing by."

A few moments later the console operator said, "The target vehicle has pulled over to the side. Driver and passenger climbing out."

Brooke watched as they opened the trunk and took out the jack and the spare. "Felix, roll. Mark, I hope this works."

"If it doesn't, I'll see you over the rainbow."

"They're moving," Gretel said. She looked at Brooke. "This is it."

Meanwhile Felix and Mark and another commando named Rolf, had swapped over to a silver 1970's Mercedes. Mark was in the back, on the passenger side. Felix passenger front. Rolf drove. Both Mark and Felix were armed with suppressed G95s.

They got back on the motorway and drove in the appropriate lane. Felix looked down at the screen in his hand of the live feed from the C-17. "One man is changing the tire, the other is watching. The trunk is open."

Mark nodded. "So far, so good."

They continued at a constant speed.

"The spare wheel is going on. How far out?"

"I can see them," the driver said.

Felix checked his weapon and slipped the fire selector from safe. "Hurry up."

In the back, Mark did the same.

Rolf put his foot down harder.

"Come on, Rolf, this is the only window we'll get before the tunnel."

The Mercedes picked up speed.

"They're putting the jack and the damaged tire away."

"We're almost there."

Felix and Mark turned their windows down and prepared to engage the two men.

Then they were there. Rolf ripped the handbrake on, and the Mercedes slid around so that Felix and Mark were facing the two men who'd just changed the tire.

Both suppressed G95s fired, and the two men jerked wildly under the impact of the rounds. They fell to the pavement and never moved.

But that was only half the job done. Felix launched himself out of the Mercedes and grabbed a fragmentation grenade. He pulled the pin and threw it into the open trunk before returning to the vehicle he'd just come from.

Rolf dropped the gas pedal to the floor and the Mercedes shot backward. A large explosion filled the front windshield, and a fireball engulfed the Audi.

Rolf stomped on the brakes and the Mercedes came to a halt. All three sat in silence looking at the burning vehicle.

It was Mark who asked, "Did we do it?"

Ortega waited impatiently for his men to change the tire. He held the trigger firmly in his grasp as he did so. One could never be too careful. He heard the two of them talking as they worked, in between vehicles flying past.

"Do you want me to get out?" Ortega called to them.

"No, sir, it is just the front."

So, he waited.

Then he heard the screech of tires and the sound of suppressed gunshots.

As Ortega looked back, he saw the armed man get out of the vehicle behind them through the gap between the Audi's body and trunk lid.

The pirate leader started to key the code in when he heard the thump in the back. He moved his thumb to hit send and just as it was coming down—

DARKNESS.

Over France

"The second team has intercepted the truck. The driver and the passenger are both dead and the load secure," Gretel said to Brooke.

Brooke let out a long sigh. "That's a relief."

"For you, maybe. I have to explain why we were conducting an operation on French soil. It isn't going to be pretty."

"Good luck with that."

"Thanks for your help. Where to now?"

Brooke thought about what she and Mark were doing before everything went sideways. "I have to go back to Sicily. Unfinished business."

"Thanks for your help."

Brooke's cell rang. She looked at the screen and said, "Sorry, I have to take this."

She hit answer and a voice asked, "Where are you?"

"Hi, Johann. Um, we're in France."

"France? What are you doing in France?"

Brooke sighed. "A lot has happened since we last talked. Sit down and hang on. This will be a ride."

22

NOT DONE YET

Sicily

Four SUVs pulled up outside the monastery. Out of the lead SUV climbed Felix, Brooke, Mark, and Rolf. From the rear one came another four commandos. Felix ordered them to set up a perimeter, and once everything was deemed clear, the doors on the remaining SUVs opened.

Johann Schmidt had discarded the sling which had been annoying him. Webster was now on crutches while Werner still had his sling. Molly and Isabella were fine. Grace was not but insisted on being there regardless.

They gathered around and Brooke escorted them towards the large doors.

"This is a creepy place," Isabella said as she looked at the carvings on the doors. Then she stopped and tilted her head to the side, looking at the eyes of the faces which were carved in the doors. "They're rubies."

"That's right," Brooke replied.

When they entered the building, realization dawned

as to why they were there. Every set of eyes went to the walls, the floor, the ceiling, just everywhere.

The change in Isabella was instant, as she became like a child in a candy store. Her eyes went wide, her heart rate elevated, and her voice was stunned. "Oh, dear Lord. This is amazing. Is it?"

"Pretty much," Brooke said with a nod. "They used the treasure to remodel."

"But how wasn't it noticed?"

"You've been to different churches. Some of them are like wonders of the world. I'm guessing that the cross was recognized and then stolen."

"With what was found after Kurt Stuber was killed, this would have to be one of the greatest finds in the world," Johann said. "Except—"

"The room?" Mark asked.

He nodded.

Brooke said, "Anika said it was in Belize with Carmen."

"Have you heard from her?" Grace asked.

Brooke shook her head. "We've heard nothing since she disappeared a week ago."

"Then you should go and look," Schmidt suggested. He looked at Felix. "Would you like to earn some extra money?"

"My guys are due a vacation."

"I'll make it worth your while. I must have that room."

He turned to Brooke. "I'll have the new jet ready to go tomorrow. Just you, Mark, and Felix's people. I don't want anyone else walking into the lion's den."

Mark smiled. "I like it. Exotic location of death."

"Would you like to stay and help Webster?" Johann asked.

The tech almost fell off his crutches. *"What?"*

Mark shook his head. "I'll take the poison darts of death."

"I thought you might."

Isabella was looking at a painting on the monastery wall. It wasn't part of the treasure as such, but it was a treasure. "This is unbelievable. I have only heard stories about this painting."

"What is it?" Mark asked.

"When Raphael started painting, he did a series of works that at the time were considered worthless. But now, even those are worth millions. Possibly more than his well-known works. This—this is one of them. Johann, look."

The billionaire walked over and stood in front of the painting. "I do believe you are right."

Isabella pirouetted and stopped, staring at a bust. "Johann, another."

"I have a feeling we could be here for a while."

———

Over France

"The second team has intercepted the truck. The driver and the passenger are both dead and the load secure," Gretel said to Brooke.

Brooke let out a long sigh. "That's a relief."

"For you, maybe. I have to explain why we were conducting an operation on French soil. It isn't going to be pretty."

"Good luck with that."

"Thanks for your help. Where to now?"

Brooke thought about what she and Mark were doing before everything went sideways. "I have to go back to Sicily. Unfinished business."

"Thanks for your help."

Brooke's cell rang. She looked at the screen and said, "Sorry, I have to take this."

She hit answer and a voice asked, "Where are you?"

"Hi, Johann. Um, we're in France."

"France? What are you doing in France?"

Brooke sighed. "A lot has happened since we last talked. Sit down and hang on. This will be a ride."

———

Carmen stared at the bloodied, filth covered figure chained to the wall in the dungeon type chamber. She nodded with contentment and said, "It appears your friends have arrived. I shall have to give them a warm welcome too."

"They are not my friends," Anika growled.

"You still have spirit; I'll give you that."

"I get it from my great grandfather."

"Your great grandfather?"

"SS-Brigadeführer Kurt Meyer."

"The murderer of prisoners and civilians?" Carmen scoffed.

"It was lies."

"I guess that's where you get it from."

"Says she whose father wants to lay waste to half of Europe."

"He is not my father?" Carmen hissed.

"Really?"

"He is a monster."

"Oh, dear." Anika's voice was condescending. "Sticks and stones."

Carmen screeched and lashed out with a clenched fist. Fresh blood flowed from Anika's mouth, and she spat it on the damp stone floor. The German woman's head came up and she gave her captor a bloody grin. "Someone has daddy issues."

"Shut your mouth."

Anika spat blood again.

Carmen turned to go, her gloating mood ruined by her prisoner. Anika watched her leave and quietly hoped that Brooke and Mark would arrive soon to help her.

———

They watched the camp for three days. There was no rush. The pirates were expecting them, and it gave the team time to observe and plan.

Carmen had at least twenty people in camp. "Just about even, I'd say," Felix said. "My boys can take them."

"It depends on what other surprises they have up their sleeves," Brooke replied, knowing it was not time to be complacent about their abilities.

"I figure that they have something below that temple," Mark said. "I've seen a few people come and go from there. One had food."

Brooke was about to say something when a voice came over their comms. "Felix, you need to take a look at this."

"Where are you?" the big man asked.

"Southwest, two hundred meters."

"Be there shortly."

Brooke said to Mark, "Keep an eye on things. We'll be back."

They slipped into the jungle and found Felix's operator standing next to some fresh mounds of dirt. Part of one had been scraped away. He pointed at it and said, "Graves."

Brooke looked down at the dirt smeared face. "I know him. Karl, one of Anika's people."

"Looks like they got involved in something."

"The question is, are they all dead or…"

"Let's find out," Felix said.

Within minutes they had the rest uncovered. Brooke said, "I don't see her."

"Which would suggest that they still have her, or that she's dead and they haven't taken the time to bury her yet," Felix replied.

Brooke ignored the last part of his suggestion and said, "Then we have to get her out."

"Do you want to?"

"She helped us when we needed it."

"Fine, let's formulate a plan and we go tonight."

———

WHAP! WHAP!

The guard dropped with two 5.56 rounds in his throat and head. Felix moved forward with Mark behind him and Brooke following them. They took shelter behind a stone building, and Felix peered around the corner across the open ground ahead of them. He was about to break cover when Mark grabbed his arm. "Wait."

"What's wrong?"

Mark pointed at the shadows across the way. Felix pulled his NVGs down and waited. It took a couple of moments but then he saw it. It was only slight, but the movement was there. "I have him."

The G95 spat and the figure disappeared.

Mark said behind him, "I have another one."

His weapon fired and a second hidden figure died.

Brooke fired and a third went down. "They've set up a trap."

Suddenly the night erupted.

"Team Two, flank right," Felix snapped. "Flank right."

As muzzle flashes lit up the night, they opened fire. Brooke fired at one of them and fell in behind cover. She dropped out her spent magazine and reloaded.

Mark stopped firing and took cover beside her. "This is fun."

A light machine gun began to clatter. Bullets chewed into stone and ricocheted off into the night. Felix took cover and said, "We have to silence that thing."

"I'll go," Mark said. "I'll flank left and get in close."

Felix reached for a grenade. "Happy Birthday."

Mark stuffed it away and started to circle around to the left using what cover he could. He got behind a stone building and almost walked into two of Carmen's men. They seemed more surprised than he was. Mark opened fire with his G95 and both men dropped.

After a deep breath, Mark continued until he could see the machine gun position. There were two men in the pit. But there were another four flanking it, two on either side. Over the comms he heard Team Two call in saying they were pinned down.

Mark reached for the grenade and pulled the pin. He counted to two and then threw it. The explosive detonated as soon as it hit the ground, the deadly blast tearing through the machine gunners and another of the flankers.

Stepping out from cover, weapon up at his shoulder, Mark fired twice, shifted target, and then fired again. Two stunned shooters fell to the ground while the remaining one sprayed bullets in his direction.

A storm of gunfire from the other commandos ripped the final gunner apart.

Felix and Brooke pressed forward. The big man slapped Mark on the shoulder. "You did well, my friend."

Brooke looked at him. "Are you alright?"

"I'm fine."

For the next ten minutes the well-trained German team cleaned out the pirates with a methodical steadiness.

"Has anyone seen Carmen?"

Felix shook his head. "No sign."

"Anika?"

Mark's turn to shake his head. "Nothing."

"Let's look around."

23

ONCE MORE INTO THE BREECH!

Belize

Anika lifted her head at the sound of gunfire. Light from out in the hallway filtered through the barred window of the iron door. After a while the gunfire died away and an uneasy quiet seemed to hang in the air, making the suddenly elevated rhythm of her heartbeat more audible.

Many minutes later the bolt on the iron door rattled and slammed back. The door groaned open, and a figure filled the doorway. Anika raised her head once more to see who it was. A familiar voice said, "I see you're just hanging around."

"About fucking time," Anika said, her throat dry. "Get me down."

Brooke said into her comms. "I have her in the third temple."

"Copy."

"And I have you both," a new voice said.

Brooke spun and saw Carmen filling the doorway. "Here I was hoping you were dead."

"I could say the same thing for you. I guess we have some unfinished business."

Carmen threw her weapon away and waited. Brooke stared at her and said, "Are we in some kind of fucking eighties movie?"

"Do you accept the challenge?"

Brooke threw her weapon down and started to rid herself of her body armor. "Fuck it."

When she was done, she loosened her shoulders and took a step towards her foe.

Behind her, Anika said, "Hey, remember me?"

Without looking back, Brooke said, "Don't go anywhere."

They came together like two trucks cannoning into each other on a freeway. Carmen drew back a fist to punch Brooke in the face, but Brooke brought her head forward catching the redhead on the cheek, splitting skin, and allowing blood to run freely towards the jawline.

Carmen reeled back and a wicked grin came to her lips. She circled Brooke and renewed her attack, feinting left before going right, catching Brooke off guard. She got her a glancing blow and Brooke staggered back. Carmen followed up with two more swift blows and a sweep of the legs which put Brooke down on the cold hard floor.

Brooke grunted and rolled away from a stomping boot. Carmen let out a howl of frustration and followed her, lashing out with a kick and catching Brooke in the ribs.

A grunt escaped from Brooke's mouth and a second kick forced air from her lungs. A third kick came but never landed. Brooke caught the boot and twisted savagely, causing her attacker to fall to the floor.

Brooke came to her feet, panting hard. She stepped forward as Carmen scrambled to her feet and returned a kick of her own.

Carmen cried out in pain and scrambled upright. She looked at Brooke with wild eyes and charged at her. Her shoulder hit Brooke in the middle and drove her back. Air whooshed as the brunette hit the wall.

Brooke brought her hands down in a double fist and slammed them into Carmen's back. Carmen grunted and hit Brooke again with her shoulder.

Brooke doubled over and Carmen hit her in the face with a clenched fist, drawing blood from her right brow. Brooke's head snapped back, and she staggered drunkenly.

Once again the redhead closed the gap and hit her in the face. Blood ran from the corner of Brooke's mouth. Through the fog of pain, she spat blood on the floor and growled, "You'll have to do fucking better than that, bitch."

With a hiss, Carmen moved again but Brooke was ready. She brought up a knee and hit Carmen in the stomach. Retching, Carmen lurched back. Brooke hit her again. Blood sprayed from Carmen's mouth.

Brooke followed her progress, and with a bloody snarl hammered her with two more blows. Carmen staggered back even further and fell to the floor of the dungeon.

Now having the advantage, Brooke stood over her only for Carmen to kick her in the stomach. As she doubled over, the redhead reached up and dragged her down by the hair.

Fire burned through Brooke's scalp as the pressure was maintained on her long hair. Carmen hit her again and Brooke sank to her knees.

Unprepared for Carmen's next movement she was surprised when she was suddenly being choked by a pair of athletic legs. Brooke struggled to free herself, but Carmen's hold was powerful. She did, however, manage to twist her head just far enough and bite down on the inside of Carmen's thigh.

The redhead let out a howl of pain and released her instantly. Brooke rolled away and came up on one knee, gasping.

Carmen did the same and coiled, ready to spring to her feet.

Then, "Brooke, where are you?"

"In here!"

Alarm came to Carmen's face. She glanced at the weapon and immediately chose flight over fight. She came to her feet and disappeared out the door into the hallway.

Brooke sat down panting. From behind her, Anika said, "You let her get away."

"Whatever."

"Get me down. I'll go after the bitch."

Brooke ignored her. Mark and Felix appeared, and the former knelt beside her, checking her over. "Are you alright?"

"The bitch got away."

"We can worry about her later."

"What about me?" Anika asked.

Mark looked up and saw her. He glanced at Felix who walked over to Anika and unchained her using a combination of bullets and brute strength. Anika stared at the big man. "Thanks."

Then she disappeared out the door.

Mark glanced at her as she left, then said to Brooke, "You have to see this."

He helped her to her feet. Outside the sun was coming up and the jungle had taken on a gray color.

They led her to a large building where they found crates stacked on crates. Mark took Brooke to the nearest one with a loose lid which he lifted and shone his flash-light inside. Brooke's eyes widened.

"We've found it."

Mark nodded eagerly with a grin. "Yes, we have."

———

Berlin, Germany, 2 Weeks Later

The last of the crates were unloaded from the truck and taken inside the old block house flak tower. Johann Schmidt turned and looked at Brooke. Her bruises were slowly disappearing, and her cuts about healed. He said, "This will be Isabella's greatest puzzle yet."

"Have you notified—"

He shook his head. "No one needs to know what we have found. Not yet."

Brooke nodded. Once the secret was out, there was no putting the genie back in the bottle. "I understand. Onto the next adventure?"

Johann nodded. "Yes, but not before you get some rest. We all need it."

"I won't say no to that," Mark replied.

The billionaire looked at Felix. "Have you considered my offer?"

"I've talked to my people. They have agreed."

Mark stared at the big commando. "Agreed to what?"

"Mister Hahn has just agreed for he and his people to become our new security force. To be called on when needed."

"Great. We're turning into a zoo and the main attrac-tion is a big shaggy bear."

Felix grinned. "Brooke, a beer to celebrate?"

"I'm in," Brooke replied.

Molly and Grace appeared. "Johann, I've almost

finished putting together the intelligence package for you."

"Thank you, Grace. Let me escort you back inside."

"Crikey, anyone would think I almost died."

Mark said, "At least you didn't have a bridge come down on you."

Johann's face grew stern. "About that…"

Mark waved a hand in the air and said, "I'm going for a coffee. Talk later."

"I'll have a black one, Mark," Molly called after him.

"Can do."

Johann looked around for Brooke who had disappeared with Felix. He turned his attention back to Grace who shrugged. "Hey, I'd run too, but I'm not up to it yet."

He smiled at her. "Let me help."

———

Mark almost walked into her, spilling the coffee. When he turned, there she was standing looking at him. "Hello, Lover."

Two weeks and no sign, yet here she was. Anika, large as life. "You look better than when I last saw you."

"I feel better."

"What are you doing in Berlin?"

Anika smiled and ignored the question. "You got the Room I see."

Mark nodded. "You saw?"

"I was watching."

"Carmen?"

"She's still out there somewhere. But I'll find her."

Mark nodded again.

Anika reached up and ran a finger over his chest, teasing. "Do you have to be somewhere?"

He held up the cardboard tray containing two coffees. "Kind of."

She gave him a seductive smile. "Ever heard of iced coffee?"

"Maybe."

"Do you like it?"

"Sometimes. Depends."

Anika leaned in close and whispered into his ear, "I'm not going to beg."

"I wouldn't expect you to."

She turned and walked away.

He watched her go.

Then followed.

IF YOU LIKED THIS, YOU MAY ALSO ENJOY: TALON!

TALON SERIES BOOK ONE

The team nobody wants, but everybody fears …

When the British government approaches the Global Corporation about stemming the flow of human trafficking across the globe, Hank Jones turns to Mary Thurston to form a team right for the job. What she pieces together is a group of misfits—no longer wanted by anyone else—with talent to burn.

Led by disgraced German Intelligence officer Anja Meyer and SAS reject Jacob Hawk, the team is autonomous, utilizing the full force of the Global Corporation and its resources, as they track across different continents in pursuit of their elusive foe—a worldwide phenomenon called Medusa.

AVAILABLE NOW

ABOUT THE AUTHOR

A relative newcomer to the world of writing, Brent Towns self-published his first book, a western, in 2015. *Last Stand in Sanctuary* took him two years to write. His first hard-cover book, a Black Horse Western, was published the following year.

Since then, he has written 26 western stories, including some in collaboration with British western author, Ben Bridges.

Also, he has written the novelization to the upcoming 2019 movie from One-Eyed Horse Productions, titled, *Bill Tilghman and the Outlaws*. Not bad for an Australian author, he thinks.

Brent Towns has also scripted three Commando Comics with another two to come.

He says, "The obvious next step for me was to venture into the world of men's action/adventure/thriller stories. Thus, Team Reaper was born."

A country town in Queensland, Australia, is where Brent lives with his wife and son.

In the past, he worked as a seaweed factory worker, a knife-hand in an abattoir, mowed lawns and tidied gardens, worked in caravan parks, and worked in the hire industry. And now, as well as writing books, Brent is a home tutor for his son doing distance education.

Brent's love of reading used to take over his life, now it's writing that does that; often sitting up until the small hours, bashing away at his tortured keyboard where he loses himself in the world of fiction.

If you're interested in sharing your thoughts in more detail, scan the QR code below! Your feedback is invaluable to me—and often helps shape my future writing endeavors.

Made in United States
Orlando, FL
03 December 2024

54921653R00167